GUNS IN THE VALLEY

The general sentiment in Mustang County was, 'This is cattle country—to hell with dirt farmers.' The citizens did not realize it, but the day of the dirt farmer was dawning and that of the cattle king and his unfenced, unlimited range was on the wane. Perhaps nobody in Mustang County but Kirk Woodward had thought deeply enough to realize this. Nobody was going to rip Woodward off—he had his six-guns and the determination to blast his opponents to hell!

GUNS IN THE VALLEY

(original title: Cow Kingdom)

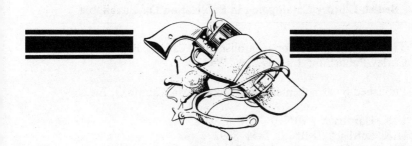

Paul Evan Lehman

ATLANTIC LARGE PRINT
Chivers Press, Bath, England.
Curley Publishing, Inc.,
South Yarmouth, Mass., USA.

Library of Congress Cataloging-in-Publication Data

Lehman, Paul Evan.
  [Cow Kingdom]
  Guns in the valley / Paul Evan Lehman.
      p.   cm.—(Atlantic large print).
  Previously published as Cow Kingdom, 1945.
  ISBN 0–7927–1123–8.
  1. Large type books.   I. Title.
[PS3523.E434C68   1992)   91–41576
813′.54—dc20.   CIP

British Library Cataloguing in Publication Data available

This Large Print edition is published by Chivers Press, England, and
Curley Publishing, Inc., U.S.A. 1992

Published by arrangement with Donald MacCampbell, Inc.

U.K. Hardback ISBN 0 7451 8380 8
U.K. Softback ISBN 0 7451 8392 1
U.S.A. Softback ISBN 0 7927 1123 8

GUNS IN THE VALLEY

CHAPTER ONE

The cowboy sat his horse in the gathering dusk, man and animal making an arresting picture against the fading light beyond the ridge on which they had halted. In a grove of cottonwoods just before them stood a sprawling ranch house. It was ablaze with light and from it came the sound of wailing violin and twanging guitar, the raised voices of men, the silvery laughter of women and the general noise of a crowd.

The cowboy shifted in his saddle and spoke softly. 'Big shindig, hoss. King Jonathan K. Lane the First is holdin' court. Crown Princess Barbara's returned from her conquest of the East, bringin' a foreigner with her named Miss Vivian Stacy, and all the dukes and lords in the kingdom are assembled to do 'em homage. Open house—except, I reckon, to nesters and rustlers, both bein' classed as one and the same in the mind of Jonathan K. Step along little hoss; trash like us got no right hangin' round the fringe of quality. Shake a foot, boy!'

At the gentle touch of steel the pony broke into the running walk which seems characteristic of the cow horse. They descended a gentle slope, following the road

1

which passed within stone throw of the JKL ranch house. The cowboy's head turned again, keen eyes searching the shadows. They discerned outbuildings and corrals, horses, spring wagons, buckboards and buggies. There were people, too: JKL punchers unhitching and corralling horses, guests moving from vehicle to house, a double file of male visitors headed to and from an open shed where four lanterns illuminated whiskey keg and beer barrel.

Opposite the house the pony halted in obedience to the tightening of the rein. The front door had opened to admit a new batch of guests and the cowboy could see the heads of people in the lighted room beyond and the sound of music and laughter was more distinct. At the entrance stood Jonathan K. Lane, and behind him was a radiant vision in pink, which could be no other than the princess. There were exclamations of pleasure, the booming voice of Lane welcoming the visitors, then the door was closed and the picture obliterated.

The cowboy abruptly reined the pony towards the cottonwoods, and as the horse hesitated, turning its head slightly as though to question, he laughed softly.

'Wonderin' what hit me, huh? Well, I don't blame you. Fact is I'm plumb curious. They say a cat can look at a queen; reckon a cowhand can take a peek at a princess. Yes, sir; I'm plumb curious to see what the East has done to her.'

He drew rein under a tree and slipped from the saddle. Big and tall he was, with the grace of the tawny puma in his movements. Tying quickly, he strode to the front entrance and rapped. As the door opened he pulled off his somewhat shabby Stetson hat.

'Howdy, Jonathan. Heard you were holdin' open house and dropped by.'

Lane's welcoming smile faded. 'Oh, it's you, Woodward. Shore, come in. Check yore gun with the sheriff over there.'

The cowboy stepped into the room, his gaze going at once to the two girls who stood a short distance away. Barbara Lane was lovely. Her skin had lost its tan and there were no signs of the freckles he remembered so well. Vivian Stacy was fair, with golden hair and blue eyes that looked at him from beneath long lashes. There was the trace of a curl to her lips, a curl which became more pronounced at sight of his worn working clothing. She raised her fan and whispered behind it to Barbara. He distinctly heard the apologetic reply: 'Kirk Woodward. He—lives near us.'

Kirk stepped forward and extended his hand. 'Howdy, Barbara. Shore am glad to have you back in God's country.'

For a moment she appeared about to take his fingers, then she glanced at Vivian and

3

caught the expression of scornful amusement on the girl's face. She stiffened, her face went into the air and her dark eyes looked clear through him. 'Good evening, Mr. Woodward.'

With a remark to Vivian about the orchestra, she turned away, and part of Kirk's question was answered. The East had indeed done something fearful and awful to Barbara Lane!

He heard a malicious chuckle to his left and turned to look at C. Hamilton Turner. Turner was the representative of an Eastern syndicate which had bought up most of the small ranches in Mustang County and had lumped them under the imposing name of The Monarch Cattle Company, Incorporated. His first name was Charles, but upon coming west he had carefully concealed that fact for fear that it might degenerate into the more vulgar Charlie or Chuck. So he had called himself C. Hamilton Turner, and, to his horror, was immediately dubbed 'Ham.' He affected an Eastern style of dress, used flawless English, and boasted the smallest, blackest, most keenly pointed and waxed mustache Mustang had ever seen.

'That was a most deliciously delivered snub, Woodward,' he said.

Kirk nodded agreement and looked at his hand. 'Maybe I forgot to wash it.'

Somebody tapped him on the arm and he

4

turned once more, this time to see Sheriff Jake Benson. Jake was a tough hombre and looked it, although he had plastered down his hair and combed his mustache until he resembled a bartender on his day off.

'Did I hear Jonathan say somethin' about checkin' yore gun?'

Kirk leisurely unbuckled the worn belt and passed it over to the officer.

'I've counted the cartridges and the holster has my initials on it. Don't make the mistake of returnin' it to somebody else, Jake.'

'You'll git yores, all right,' promised the sheriff; then added meaningly, 'And you can take that any way you want to.' Jake, owing his office to Jonathan Lane, had no use for the Woodwards.

Sauntering to a corner, Kirk dropped into a chair, tilted it against the wall and gazed about him. The party was quite patently dedicated to the upper crust of Mustang society. It was not at all like one of the good old-fashioned shindigs which seemed to typify the very spirit of the West. There were a few cowboys present, seated uncomfortably on the edges of chairs or leaning awkwardly against the walls, but they were utterly overlooked and spent most of their time moving to or from the liquor shed.

Couples were being assembled for a square dance. Ham Turner had appropriated Barbara and was bowing over her hand. It

5

was an extravagant gesture and the girl's cheeks flushed as she realized that Kirk's mocking gaze was upon her. Vivian Stacy was paired with Judge Kelly, corpulent dean of Lane's political henchmen. He was wearing a swallowtail coat almost as old as himself, which consequently failed to meet in front by about eight inches. Kirk grinned at remembrance of the chant the kids of Mustang had originated: *'Old Judge Kelly with the big fat belly!'*

Kirk got up and walked slowly along the wall, exchanging greetings with the cowboys he passed. Going through the dining room, he thrust his head around the kitchen doorway. Several Mexican women were preparing food under the direction of Barbara's younger sister, Nellie. She exclaimed at sight of him. 'Kirk Woodward! Haven't seen you in a coon's age, cowboy. How are you?'

Kirk grinned. He liked Nellie; she was human. 'Fine as frog feathers. How's pore little Cinderella?'

Nellie was not as pretty as her sister, but when she looked at Kirk her face invariably softened and a warm light came into her brown eyes.

'Somebody has to do the chores, but if you ask me I might find time for one dance.'

He shook his head regretfully. 'Reckon I'll have to decline the honor. I like you too much, lady, to drag you down to my humble level. The air in the front room is plumb full of upturned noses.'

Nellie tossed her dark curls. 'The stuck-ups! Well, if you won't dance, at least you'll stay to sample some of my cooking.'

'Nope, I'm on my way. Just wanted to say howdy to you.'

'You're not going away empty-handed, then. I'll wrap up a piece of chocolate cake for you to take along. Now what—?'

From without came a sudden clamor, a crescendo of sound that silenced the music and sent the guests scurrying to doors and windows: shrill yells, the thunder of pounding hoofs, the bellowing roar of six-guns.

Kirk leaped to the back door and flung it open. A body of riders swept through the yard, orange lances of flame cutting the darkness. Straight for the wagon shed and its illuminated kegs they charged, the men who were tasting Lane's hospitality scattering before them. Ropes encircled the posts of the open structure, there came a rending of wood and the screech of nails, and the roof came down atop the barrels. Oil from the lanterns caught fire and in a few minutes the wreckage was ablaze.

With wild yells of glee, the riders made for the night corral. In this inclosure were the horses of the JKL cowboys and their guests. The big gate was opened and the animals within were liberated and driven out on the range. With a final whoop and a volley of six-gun fire, the band made off, leaving behind them the blazing shed and empty corral.

Kirk stepped aside to permit the exit of a stream of sweating men. They found buckets and a couple of them manned the pump. Desperately they threw water on the flames, now tinged with an alcoholic blue. In vain; despite their best efforts the fire gained headway and at last even the thirstiest and most optimistic of them had to concede the loss of their liquid refreshment.

It was then that they thought of pursuit, only to find the corral empty. Except for Kirk's horse and three blooded saddle mounts stabled in the barn, not one remained at ranch headquarters.

Kirk re-entered the kitchen to be faced by a stormy-eyed Nellie.

'I like fun, but that was a downright mean trick!' she declared. 'I suppose Tom was at the bottom of it.'

'Nellie, I give you my word I know nothin' about it.'

'Of course you don't. But that wild, reckless brother of yours! Why don't you try to do something with him?'

'I was sort of leavin' that to you,' answered Kirk slyly.

'It's high time somebody did something

with him!'

It was Barbara who had spoken, and her angry gaze was upon Kirk. By her stood Vivian Stacy and Ham Turner. Kirk surveyed her calmly, paying no attention to the other two. His steady gaze infuriated the girl.

'Why do you stare at me? You heard what I said. Tom Woodward leads these night riders. Everybody knows it.'

'If Tom was in that bunch it's because he feels that you had somethin' like this comin' to you. All they destroyed was an old wagon shed; you big outfits burn crops, destroy fences, kill the home steaders' cattle if they happen to stray. I'd say they let you off easy.'

Jonathan Lane and Sheriff Benson had pushed through the doorway in time to hear this. Lane's face was ruddy with wrath and he spoke heatedly.

'And why do we do it, huh? I'll tell you why! This is cattle country; always was and always will be. We ranchers came in here and fought Indians and rustlers and outlaws to build our homes and raise our cows. It's our range! Then along come you dirt farmers, to plow up the grass and grab our pasture. You keep crowdin' us, cuttin' down our grazin' and takin' our water, pushin' us farther and farther back! When you get hungry for beef you shoot our yearlin's, take what you want, and leave the rest for the buzzards. That's why we burn yore crops and tear down yore

9

fences. And, by Godfrey! that's what we aim to keep on doin' until everyone of you thievin' nesters is driven plumb outa the country!

Kirk's steady gaze did not falter. 'Seems to me like you're takin' in too much territory, Jonathan. We ain't all thieves and dirt farmers. My father came in here almost as soon as you did. And we don't farm, we run cows the same as the JKL, although it's a losin' proposition with you big fellers classin' us with rustlers and trash.'

Ham Turner, feeling that there was safety in numbers, had to deliver himself. 'Men are judged by the company they keep. Look at the trash your brother associates with—Shab Townsend, Rum Blossom Bates, Joel Cord—all thieves or worse.'

'You better keep out of this, Ham. Lane can talk free because he's an old-timer and should know what he's talkin' about. You came out here not knowin' a honda from a post hole and with nothin' behind you but lousy syndicate gold. It was yore Monarch outfit that started this war, runnin' off homesteaders, takin' by force what you couldn't buy. But the Woodwards don't scare easy, and we wouldn't sell to you to save ourselves from starvin'.'

'No danger of that,' sneered Turner. 'Not with honest men's cattle so handy and reprobates like Tom Woodward on the loose.'

Kirk took two strides forward, his eyes blazing at the insult. Ham shrank back, but not in time. A hand swept in a short arc and its leathery palm caught him squarely on the cheek with a resounding smack. Instantly Kirk leaped backward, his left hand tearing at his shirt. Sheriff Jake Benson was going for his gun!

The buttons flew from Kirk's shirt, his right hand snaked in and came out holding a Derringer. 'Hold it, Jake!' he cried.

But Jake had started his draw and had to go through with it. He fired from the hip, and Kirk felt the tug of the bullet even as he released the hammer of his own gun. Benson's arm went suddenly limp and he staggered back against the door frame. Behind Jake, Kirk could see the languid looking, soft-spoken Virgil Depew dragging two guns from shoulder holsters. His own Derringer fired but two shots and only one of these remained.

He leaped straight at Jonathan Lane, swinging him about and jamming the barrel of his gun against Lane's back. 'Jonathan, stop them! Godfrey, man, there are women in the room! You hear me? Stop them!'

Men had rushed for their checked guns and now were coming at a run. Lane, fearing for the safety of his daughters and his guests, started shouting.

'Stop it, everybody! Damn it, Benson, stop

them! The next man that fires a shot will settle with me!'

Barbara and Vivian had flattened themselves against the wall. Now into the cleared doorway came Virg Depew, crouched, gliding, face twisted into the savage mask of the paid killer. Behind him was Stoney Stone. They were Ham Turner's pet gunmen. Both had drawn.

'Virg! Stone! Put up those guns! I said *put up those guns!*'

Depew flashed one glance towards Ham Turner, who nodded. Instantly the mask changed; Depew straightened and the guns disappeared as quickly as they had come into sight. Jonathan Lane wheeled to face Kirk.

'I might have known you'd pull somethin' like this! You come here uninvited and accept my hospitality and all the while you were packin' a gun.'

'Good thing I was,' said Kirk tranquilly. 'Looks like I'd 'a' been the only one without one. As for hospitality, all of you except Nellie have tried to make me feel like a skunk at a prayer meetin'. You reckon I can leave without bein' plugged in the back?'

'Damn you, yes! You're safe while you're under my roof.'

Kirk holstered the Derringer, drew his shirt together and walked past Barbara into the front room. There was the silence of death as he stalked to the wall and got his

12

gunbelt and hat. At the front door he turned and made a mocking bow to the girls, who had followed him into the room.

'My respects, ladies,' he said politely. 'Also my apologies, Barbara, I say again that I'm glad you came back to God's country. I shore hope it isn't too late.'

The door closed behind him and for a moment there was silence; then Barbara, her eyes bright with anger, walked quickly to the entrance, opened the door and went out after him. He had mounted his horse, but at sight of her upraised hand drew rein and looked calmly down at her.

'I just wanted to tell you,' she said tightly, 'how thoroughly contemptible I think you.'

He eyed her curiously, as though examining some particularly interesting specimen of the animal kingdom. 'Barbara, I'm goin' to tell you somethin'. I horned in on yore party just to see what the East had done to you. You see, I remembered a little girl who was unspoiled and spunky and who used to take long rides with me. She wasn't such a han'some girl, Barbara; her face was freckled and her nose sorta turned up at the end, but she had a heart of gold and was a mighty good pal. Now—well, her nose still turns up and I'm not denyin' her spunk. That's about all I can say. Was a time when I swore I was goin' to marry her when she grew up. I know now that I was plumb crazy.'

13

'Why, you—you insulting *cad!*'

He was unmoved. 'That's a new word to me; reckon you picked it up in the East. As for insults, that reminds me I got one to repay.'

He leaned swiftly from the saddle and she felt herself lifted from her feet. So surprised was she that she did not resist. He kissed her, kissed her on the lips with a force that she was to feel for hours afterwards. Then he set her gently on the ground, and horse and man were swallowed by the darkness. But his last disgusted words remained with her.

'Face powder! Now I know what become of the freckles.'

Barbara stood there glaring after him, fists clenched, tears of anger and mortification on her lashes. From behind her came the voice of Vivian, who, unobserved, had followed her outside.

'Well! He certainly read *your* pedigree! What an astonishing man! I wonder why he didn't seize you by the hair and drag you away to his cave?'

CHAPTER TWO

Kirk Woodward rode slowly along the road which led from Mustang to his father's homestead on the far side of the valley. Ahead of him, just a few minutes before, had sped the band of riders which had partly spoiled Barbara's homecoming party by destroying the liquor supply and then had added insult to injury by turning out the horses of crew and guests.

Nellie had accused Tom Woodward of being the leader of these wild spirits, and Kirk was forced to admit that she was probably right. Tom was a likable kid, but filled with the Old Nick and teeming with resentment at the way the big cattlemen treated the homesteaders. It was quite possible that he had banded together other young blades of the community for the purpose of harassing the cattlemen in every way possible.

Both cowman and homesteader felt justified in his antagonism for the other. The belief of the former had been aptly stated by Jonathan Lane that very evening. The homesteader held that the land upon which the cattleman grazed his stock was not his; it belonged to the public domain and the cowman was, therefore, a trespasser. The homesteader applied for his land and earned title to it by clearing and developing it and remaining on it for the required length of time. He had the law on his side, but the law was often too remote or too indifferent to furnish him protection.

In some cases, as in Mustang County, the

law was owned outright by the cattleman. Sheriff Jake Benson was Lane's man; so was Judge Kelly. When a homesteader appealed for help he found Benson busy with more important things and the judge absent on some mysterious business. The town of Mustang was Lane's; he had built it and kept it going in the early days. The citizens were quite content, feeling more secure under the benevolent domination of a rich, influential cattleman than they would have under a dozen or more poverty-stricken nesters. The general sentiment was, 'This is cattle country—to hell with dirt farmers.' They did not realize it, but the day of the dirt farmer was dawning and that of the cattle king and his unfenced, unlimited range on the wane.

Perhaps nobody in Mustang County but Kirk Woodward had thought deeply enough to realize this. Kirk was by nature and inclination a cattleman; he was an expert with the tools of his trade, he thrilled to the surge of a speeding horse beneath him and the rush of wind in his face. But he was a discerning young man and he saw that the dirt farmer must come, and no amount of cattle barons with their hard-bitten crews could stop him.

There was another contributing cause to the passing of the cattle king. The old-timers like Jonathan Lane were dying off; ranches were being bought up by Eastern syndicates like the Monarch outfit. These corporations, more than a thousand miles away, had to depend upon resident managers who were often enough ignorant of the cattle business or dishonest or both. Against these inefficients the cattle rustlers rose *en masse*, often encouraged if not actually aided by the homesteaders. Such was the state of affairs on the Mustang range.

Kirk remained on JKL range all the way to the Woodward boundary. Lane's land was still unfenced except across its southern boundary where the Monarch had run a line of wire stretching from the hills on the west to the small creek, most of the time dry, which ran northward towards the distant Gila. This creek paralleled the western mountains, along the foot of which had existed a string of homesteads. Except for those of Woodward and several others to the north, these claims had been bought by the Monarch or appropriated by them after their owners had been run off; consequently the ranch managed by C. Ham Turner extended across the valley to the south of the JKL and thence northward on the east side of the creek as far as the Flying W.

Woodward and his sons had thus far resisted every effort of the M to oust them. The M wanted their land because of a fine spring which was the source of a small stream flowing across the homestead and into the creek. Its possession would have permitted

17

the syndicate to expand even farther north. Lane, who had all the range he needed, sided with the Monarch for the simple reason that he detested all nesters.

Kirk's horse finally descended the west bank of the creek and stopped to drink of the overflow of the Flying W water hole. To the south of this point the bed of the creek was dry. And while he sat his saddle waiting, there came to him sounds which caused him to snap erect and cock his ears to the south. Somewhere down there cattle were on the creek.

It was not difficult to guess what had happened. Profiting by the party on the JKL, rustlers had descended upon Lane's range and were driving some of his beef into Mexico. The feeling between homesteaders and cattlemen being what it was, Kirk ordinarily would not have interfered; but tonight it was different. Tom was on the loose and there was the chance that the theft of Lane's stock might be one of his ideas of good clean fun.

Kirk turned his horse down the creek bed and put him to a lope; but before he had covered a mile he heard the sound of approaching hoofs and the ring of iron on stone which bespoke horses. He reined his pony to the left and sent him lunging up the east bank and into the shadow of a cottonwood.

18

A band of horsemen swept by at a lope and he knew at once that these were the riders who had raided the JKL. His face relaxed slightly. No matter what other mischief was afoot, at least these wild bucks were not engaged in rustling. The band continued to the Flying W boundary, then returned, passing Kirk at a walk, talking and laughing among themselves. Kirk urged his horse to the creek bed and followed them.

At the M fence the gully curved towards the Monarch ranch house, and here the party left it, striking off towards a squalid settlement known as Bate's Bottom. This was a collection of shacks and dives inhabited by scum from both sides of the border.

Kirk followed at a discreet distance and presently his horse was picking its way along the dim trail which led to the Bottom, where a few feeble lights marked the location of Rum Blossom Bates' saloon. Swinging to the ground in front of the place, Kirk left his horse with the others and entered. Tom and his companions were lined up before the makeshift bar, drinking. Rum Blossom was not in evidence, nor were any of the other usual denizens of the saloon, and Kirk had a fairly clear idea of the kind of business which had called them away.

He sat down on a box and proceeded to roll a cigarette, and presently was espied by his brother, Tom. 'Well, if it ain't old

19

sobersides!' cried the boy. 'Kirk, what in Goshen steered you to this dump?'

'Just moseyin' around. Heard a lot of fellers exercisin' their hosses and got thirsty tryin' to figure out what they were doin'. Is that stuff the boys are pourin' out good to drink?'

'No, but it shore cuts the dust. Want to try it?' Tom extended a tincupful of the stuff to Kirk, who drained it with a wry face.

Tom grinned and pulled up another box. 'Kirk, we've had the dangdest time! Waited until old JKL's party got goin', then rode into the yard, pulled down his liquor shed and turned the hosses out of the corral. Haw! They were hoppin' mad, but they'd checked their guns and we got plumb away.'

'Yeah, I know. I was there.'

Tom stared. 'You were there? *You?*'

'Uh-huh. Got curious to see what kind of a shindig they were throwin'.'

'And they didn't kick you out?'

'Well, they come close to it. I left by general request, but under my own steam. Boy, don't ever go East. It's bad medicine. Look at Ham Turner. And Barbara—the little freckle-face gal we used to know—you oughta see what it done to her. All powdered up, dressed like a duchess, chin in the air. Called me a cad.'

'What's that? Some kinda new cuss-word?'

'I ain't shore, but it's no compliment . . .

20

Well, you boys done a good job of coverin' up cattle tracks, didn't you?'

Tom gave him a swift glance. 'What do you mean?'

'I heard cattle traipsin' down the creek bed—heard 'em a mile off. Then yore bunch came tearin' up the trail clear to the Flyin' W and back again. I ride over here and find Rum Blossom and Shab and Joel Cord and the rest of the bunch missin'. It don't take a college education to figure that they drove off some JKL steers and that you covered their tracks for 'em.'

'You're too danged smart. But what of it? Lane shoots our stock if they stray across the creek. I'd like to see him robbed blind!'

'Shore you would; but stealin' is stealin' no matter how you look at it, and the Woodwards were never rustlers. Also they're gettin' wise to this night-ridin' gang of yores. Everybody on the JKL had you tagged as the leader of that raidin' party; if they find out that they lost some cows, they'll hang that onto you, too. Ham Turner has already hooked you up with Shab and Joel and Rum Blossom.'

'The danged stuck-up tenderfoot! I'll take that out of his hide when I catch up with him. I ain't no thief, that's one thing certain.'

Kirk laid a hand on his brother's knee. 'Shore you ain't! But the fellers you run around with are thieves and maybe worse. We

21

know it, but we don't give them away because they're fightin' the men that are fightin' us ... Well, I'll be amblin' along. Just watch yore step, boy.'

Tom followed him to the door. 'Didn't happen to see Nellie, did you?'

'Shore did. She wanted to wrap up some cake for me but I didn't have time to wait for it. She's the best one in the outfit. She—mentioned you.'

'She did? Say! She's all right.'

'She'll make some man a fine wife, but he'll have to be a square-shooter and honest and—steady. I'll be seein' you.'

He rode home the way he had come. Tom cared for Nellie in his wild, reckless way, but what the girl thought of him Kirk did not know. She might be the restraining influence his younger brother needed.

★   ★   ★

At the breakfast table the next morning Asa Woodward gave them their instructions for the day. 'The south fence is down in several places. You boys take care of it; I'll patch up the east line. Tom, you take the end nearest the creek; Kirk can look after the middle. If you find—'

He broke off as the kitchen door opened. A man entered timidly, an old derelict of a man, the shabbiest, most forlorn creature that could be imagined. From the tattered hat down the ragged and multipatched shirt and overalls to the worn boots with their run-over heels he was the picture of poverty and decay.

His scraggly gray hair was long and dirty, his cheeks and chin were covered with a grimy stubble many days old, and the ragged mustache drooped dejectedly to match a toothless and trembling mouth and a pair of sad, watery blue eyes.

'Mornin', gents,' he mumbled. 'Reckon yuh c'n spare me a mite to eat?'

'Howdy, Tanglefoot,' answered Kirk. 'Drag up a chair and pitch in.'

'Thankee, Kirk, thankee kindly.' He dropped his hat to the floor and shuffled to the table with a chair. He began eating like a half-starved wolf, but presently paused and looked from one to another impressively. 'Boys, I reckon I'm a-goin' to find her.'

The three paid little attention. It was an old story to them. Years before, Tanglefoot Tarberry had stumbled on a ledge rich with gold. So rotten with ore was it that he could pick up the virgin gold from the top of the ground. But according to his story, he had been at the end of his resources, with his water almost gone, so he gathered a sackful of the stuff, loaded it on his burro and started for Mustang.

In some way he became lost and in crossing a stretch of desert had come near to

23

perishing. His burro died and he staggered on alone. Finally reaching Mustang, he lingered only long enough to recuperate before starting back for the spot where he had left burro and gold. He found neither; the vultures and the shifting sand had taken care of that.

Desperately he sought to find somebody who would believe his story to the extent of grubstaking him for a search, and finally Kirk, out of sheer pity for the old fellow, had purchased him an outfit and had accompanied him on what proved to be a fruitless journey.

That was three years before, and since then Tanglefoot had been begging grubstakes and wandering about in the hills. At last his mind weakened and now he was a harmless old coot, a pest and a nuisance whom nester and rancher fed and sent on his way in order that he might not die on their hands. And always he was just on the verge of making his big discovery.

'Yes, sir,' he went on eagerly, 'the next time I'm a-goin' to find her. One more grubstake's all I need, that's all. Jest one more grubstake.'

He looked about him hopefully but saw no glitter of anticipation in the eyes that regarded him. With a weary sigh he resumed eating.

Asa Woodward and Tom arose from the table and started for work, leaving Kirk to get rid of the old man. Kirk washed up the dishes while Tanglefoot finished eating, then gave him a pipeful of tobacco and put a question. 'Where you headin' from here, old-timer?'

Tanglefoot eyed him wistfully. 'I wisht I was a-headin' fer my lost ledge. I know I c'n find her now! Kirk, yuh allus been good to me, good to a old, throwed-away man that nobody else has a kind word fer. Yuh was my poddner onct, Kirk. Gosh a'mighty, boy, if yuh would jest grubstake me onct more! We'd be rich, rich as Midas! I tell yuh, that there gold lays in piles jest fer the pickin' up! I see it in m' dreams and it plumb ha'nts me! A-layin' there, she is, waitin' fer me! Kirk, I've tried everywhere to git me a grubstake, but I'm jest a old throwed-away man and they won't listen to me. Kirk, yuh ain't gonna turn me down, be yuh?'

There was a pathetic tremble in the cracked voice; the watery blue eyes searched Kirk's face with the hopeful eagerness of an old, half-starved hound beseeching its master for a moldy bone. A deep pity stirred Kirk. Without a word he went to the fireplace and withdrew a stone from the hearth. From the opening he took a small sack and emptied its contents on the table. It contained possibly a hundred dollars in coins. Gravely he divided it into two piles and pushed one of them over to the old man. Tanglefoot pounced upon it with exultant cries of appreciation.

'Thankee, Kirk! Oh, thankee! I tell yuh,

we'll be rich as Midas!'

'Tanglefoot, it will be the last grubstake from me. I've outfitted you again and again out of the little I've saved. Usually you drink it up at Bates' Bottom, but I've never complained. This is the end; I just cain't waste what little I got helpin' you get yore feet so's they won't track.'

'I won't spend a dime of it fer liquor, Kirk! I swear I won't!'

'All right. Mosey along. That'll buy you a burro and enough grub to last a month. Stretch it out, Tanglefoot.'

When the old man had gone, Kirk caught up his horse and rode to the south boundary of the Flying W. Here he set about repairing fence. For an hour he worked steadily; then, from somewhere in the direction of the creek, came the spiteful crack of a rifle.

Kirk leaped for his horse. Tom was working down there, and with a war on between cattleman and homesteader anything might have happened. He followed the fence, dragging out his Winchester as he rode. Presently he came to the brakes, a tangled mass of chaparral and stunted trees which obstructed the view and hindered progress. When he finally broke through to the bank of the creek a tense scene was revealed.

Below him, in the creek bed, lay a dead cow. Even at the distance he could read the JKL on her flank. Standing by his horse near her was Tom, his hands in the air, and covering him with his six-gun was Jonathan Lane. Off to one side the two girls sat their horses, and the remaining member of the party, C. Hamilton Turner, had just leveled his rifle at Kirk.

'Drop your rifle!' ordered Ham sharply.

Kirk promptly dropped the Winchester and raised his hands.

'Now ride down here, and ride slowly.'

'Reckon you got me where you want me,' said Kirk. 'Wait a minute till I untangle this stirrup.'

As he spoke he leaned to his right, reaching down. Lane's sharp warning to Turner came too late. Slipping his left foot free, Kirk dived into the brush squarely beside the rifle, and the next moment its barrel was poked through the branches and aimed at the bewildered and chagrined Turner.

'Now you can drop yores,' said Kirk, and Ham hastily obeyed.

Kirk got to his feet and slid down the bank, rifle held at the ready. Lane was berating Ham for his stupidity; he, himself, could do nothing. If he shifted his gun to cover Kirk, Tom would be free to draw. Assured that Turner was no longer a menace, Kirk swung the rifle to cover Lane.

'You can put up yore gun, Jonathan,' he said, and when Lane had done so he lowered the rifle and gazed at the cow. The animal had

27

been shot through the head and lay on the Woodward side of the line which divided the two spreads. He looked up at Barbara. 'Reckon you folks are goin' to have beef stew for dinner.'

'It's too bad we were so close,' she answered tartly. 'No doubt you would have enjoyed a nice, juicy tenderloin yourself.'

'Off that critter? Lady, she's a cow, and an old one at that. But then you wouldn't know—havin' been educated in the East.'

Lane interrupted harshly. 'This is one time you're not goin' to put it over on us, Woodward. That cow was shot on my side of the line and dragged over to the Flyin' W.'

'There's nothin' wrong with my eyesight, Jonathan; but you're too quick at jumpin' at conclusions. You can see that Tom's rope is coiled and tied to his saddle, and he ain't even carryin' a rifle.'

'It don't take long to wind up a rope, and he could throw the rifle into the brush.'

'I tell you I didn't do it!' blazed Tom. 'I was workin' fence and heard the shot. I got here just before you did.'

'That's what *you* say!' sneered Ham.

Kirk regarded him coldly. 'If experience is a good teacher, Ham, you shore are a dumb pupil. This is a JKL cow; after last night I thought you'd know enough to keep yore mouth shut in affairs that don't concern you.'

Ham's face darkened. 'I'll repay you for

28

that blow, my friend.'

'Don't call me your friend. You hate me from the ground up and I return the compliment, double.' He looked Lane in the eyes. 'Jonathan, the sign should read right plain to an old-timer like you. That cow was shot and dragged over the line by somebody who seen you comin' and who wanted to make trouble between us. An old hand like you shore ain't goin' to be fooled by such a clumsy trick. If we were hungry for beef, we'd shore know enough to pick a nice fat yearlin' instead of a grass-eater like that.'

For a moment longer Lane glared at him, but the logic of what Kirk had said was not to be denied. He turned to his horse. 'I'll send a man down to dress her out,' he mumbled, and mounted.

Turner picked up his rifle and followed suit, for once holding his tongue. The two girls lingered a moment and Barbara spoke scathingly.

'You're very sure of yourself, aren't you, Mr. Woodward?'

Kirk grinned. 'I just cain't help it,' he admitted, and waved an arm in a motion which embraced the whole landscape. 'Born and raised and educated in the wild, untrammeled spaces of my native West! No waxed mustache, no slicked-down hair, no starched shirt—and plenty of freckles!'

'Beast!'

'Is that higher or lower than a cad?'

Barbara's face was tight. 'Come on, Vivian. We can't waste time on a miserable nester.'

But Vivian Stacy was leaning from her saddle, her cheeks dimpled in a smile, her languid eyes warm and tempting. She spoke softly. 'Don't mind Barbara, Mr. Woodward. I don't agree with her at all. I think you're splendid!'

'Why—thanks!' gasped the amazed Kirk.

'Oh, come on, Vivian!' cried the exasperated Barbara. 'What in the world do you know about the West?'

'Well,' murmured Vivian sweetly, 'at least I recognized that defunct animal as a cow!'

CHAPTER THREE

C. Hamilton Turner had dinner at the JKL, delighting Barbara with his good manners and genteel conversation. It was plain to her that C. Hamilton was a man of culture and refinement, with a knowledge of art and literature which left her amazed and a bit awed. She had no means of knowing that he was playing a game in accordance with a dazzling plan which he had suddenly conceived.

Jonathan Lane smelled a rat but wasn't sure just yet that it was Ham. He said very little during the meal, but his speculative gaze rested often on the Easterner when that person was not aware of it. It occurred to Lane that Turner might be spreading himself in order to impress Barbara, and he did not know whether or not to be flattered. Turner was apparently well-to-do and undoubtedly possessed more than his share of wit and education, but Jonathan was of the rough old school which had little sympathy or respect for those who earned their bread with their brains rather than by good honest toil.

Ham was astute enough to leave early, and he left with Barbara's sincere invitation to call again very soon. The girl liked books and art and Ham was the only one who could talk intelligently to her of them. Vivian was her guide in gentility and style, but at the moment she did not feel kindly towards the girl who had gone out of her way to pay compliments to Kirk Woodward. Kirk had infuriated her and at the same time had shamed her, and Vivian, instead of resenting this had actually seemed pleased.

Once Ham left the JKL ranch house his veneer of good nature vanished. His pride still smarted under the scathing remarks of Kirk Woodward just as his cheek continued to tingle from the fellow's hard palm. He had been humbled in the eyes of both girls and this he could never forgive.

The sleepy-eyed, tigerish Virgil Depew and

the stolid Stoney Stone rode behind him, for
Ham never ventured abroad alone. From the
moment he had assumed control of the
Monarch holdings he had made enemies. His
first act had been to hire a tough crew, most
of them drawn from Bates' Bottom, all
hard-riding, swift-shooting hombres who
knew neither fear nor compassion. His
foreman was Sergeant Gault, an adventurer
who had fought in half a dozen armies south
of the line and who combined the ruthlessness
of the western desperado with the discipline
of the soldier. He rodded the crew with a
stern hand, exacting implicit and instant
obedience. They called him 'Sarge.'

With such an outfit as this to back him,
Ham started warring with the homesteaders
who had settled on the east side of the creek
at the base of the Mustang range of hills.
Their fences were systematically destroyed,
their crops trampled, their homes burned. In
vain they appealed to the law; Sheriff Jack
Benson was Lane's man and shared with him
a hatred of all nesters. In the end, most of
these homesteaders, wearied of the constant
fight for existence, sold out to Ham for almost
nothing; others, more stubborn, fought on
until ruined and driven out of the valley. The
Woodwards gathered their neighbors to the
north and made a determined stand. In one
pitched battle they crippled the Monarch
forces so badly that even the doughty Gault

was forced to concede them the victory and pull his men back to the M to lick their wounds.

Thus matters stood when Ham reached the creek at the Woodward boundary and, crossing it, turned south. The hurt to his pride was tempered by the knowledge that the ground he trod was his. He had bought it with Monarch money and steers wearing the M grazed upon it, but title reposed in his name. At the start he had warned the officer of the Monarch syndicate that there would probably be no profit for the first year or two, owing to difficulties with rustlers and nesters. They had believed him, and Ham immediately took care to see that his prediction was realized.

On the far side of the hills along whose base he rode was another ranch also purchased with Monarch funds and without official Monarch knowledge. It was managed by a man called Cliff Venner and the brand he registered was a Box V. His name was not really Venner, but Ham had found it convenient to call him that because the initial V lent itself beautifully to the scheme of things. By closing the top and bottom of the Monarch M with two strokes of a running iron a Box V was formed. The operation was foolproof because of its simplicity, and the loss in stock accounted for in Ham's reports as due to the depredations of rustlers was represented by a corresponding increase in the herd of Cliff Venner.

Sarge Gault was on the gallery cleaning a rifle when Ham and his two bodyguards rode into the yard. He greeted Turner with a brief nod and an equally brief statement. 'Venner's inside.'

'Good!' Ham turned his horse over to Stoney Stone and mounted the steps. 'Come in, Sarge. I've something I want to talk over with you.'

Inside the house they found a lean, horsefaced man who sat in a big chair with one long leg draped over an arm of it. His hat was balanced on his knee in order that he might lean back in comfort. 'Hy-yuh, Ham,' he greeted.

Turner winced. 'Stop calling me that! If you can't pronounce the full name, call me Turner. Come into the office, both of you.'

He led the way into a small room at one end of the building, dropped into a swivel chair behind his desk and motioned to chairs.

'How's the stuff in the southeast pasture, Sarge?'

'Every last one of 'em's healed up. Venner can drive whenever he wants to.'

'Drive 'em tonight,' said Venner promptly. 'Figgered they might be ready, but what I really come over for was to get me some money. Pay-day's comin' up and I'm short.'

'I'll take care of it before you leave.

34

Everything going well on your side of the hills?'

'Everything goin' smooth as silk. Changin' a M to a Box V is so danged easy that a stock inspector wouldn't catch it less'n he turned the hide inside out. Had a buyer lookin' at them yearlin's last week. All prime stuff and he'll give us top price. Ham—I mean, Turner—yuh're gonna git rich if the Monarch stuff holds out.'

Turner frowned. He didn't like to share his secrets with men of the caliber of Venner, but in this case it couldn't be helped. 'There's a limit, of course, but with all the rustlers and homesteaders I've reported as preying on us I can hold out for some time yet. Now if you'll excuse us, Cliff, I want to talk with Gault. Make yourself at home and when we get through I'll fix up that payroll for you.'

The horsefaced man unlimbered and ambled from the room, and Gault carefully closed the door behind him. Turner lowered his voice.

'Any news from last night's drive?'

'Ain't had time yet, but everything should be jake. We helped the boys haze the stuff down to the line and young Woodward's gang covered the tracks for us.'

'Rather paradoxical situation, isn't it, to have our enemies working for us?'

'I don't know what that word means, but I get yore general drift. Young Woodward

35

helps the Bottom boys because he thinks they're stealin' from us, too. How you make out over that dead cow?'

Ham's face darkened at the memory. 'Badly. That damned Kirk Woodward had to show up and spoil the thing.' He acquainted Gault with the details. 'He's made me appear ridiculous on several occasions lately, and I promised him I'd make him pay for it.'

'He's a smart feller. If anything happens to him it better be through the JKL. You got a whole school of fish on yore hooks and you gotta be shore you don't get yore lines snarled.'

Ham grinned. 'I've hooked another one within the last twenty-four hours, and it's a whale.'

'Yeah? What is it this time?'

Ham withheld nothing from Sarge Gault. It was necessary to the success of his scheme that he have one man on whom he could rely, a man who in an emergency could take up the reins and carry on knowing where he was going. Ham had wisely chosen Gault. The man had been a soldier, was disciplined, a hard driver, and could keep his counsel. Turner spoke freely.

'That's what I wanted to talk to you about. You know the original idea. There is money in cattle if things are managed right. My intention was and still is to build a big spread, the largest in Mustang County. Right now we

36

have the Box V and the homesteads east of the creek as far north as the Woodward property. When we get the Flying W—which we will—it will be an easy matter to run out the nesters north of there. Then I'll inform the syndicate that the Monarch has been so depleted that it is no longer advisable to hold on to it, and recommend that they sell.'

'Which is where I step in,' said Gault. 'I buy the outfit for a song—with you furnishin' the words and music.'

'As well as the cash,' added Turner. 'It's a pleasant prospect, isn't it?'

'It's a gold mine!'

'Think so? Well, listen to this. So far we haven't considered the JKL seriously, merely contenting ourselves with a cut in the profits earned by the Bottom boys. Their stuff must be disposed of south of the line, for not even an expert like yourself can change a JKL into an M or a Box V. The Bottom fellows get the gravy, but our cut comes in handy; however, I've decided that it isn't enough.'

'Them buzzards won't stand for givin' us a bigger slice,' said Gault.

'I don't want a mere slice ... Is that door closed tightly?'

Gault went over, opened the door and looked out, then closed it and locked it. When he had reseated himself, Ham went on.

'Lane is a power; he owns the law and the town of Mustang. Everybody jumps when he

37

cracks the whip. Gault, I want his place, I want his power, I want to wrest control of the whole country from him! It would make us, man! We'd be sitting on top of the world.'

Gault drew a deep breath. 'So that's yore whale! Man, yuh'll never land it. Yuh're bitin' off too big a chunk. Lane's been established too long; he's too big for yuh to budge.'

'Yes? Listen!' Ham leaned across the desk in his eagerness. 'Lane's daughter, Barbara, came home yesterday. Sarge, she's a looker! I spent half a day talking books and art with her and I'm sure I made a good impression. If I were to marry her I'd be heir to half of that big spread. And if Lane were to check out before Nellie is of age I'd probably be made administrator of her half too. I'd have Mustang under my thumb, together with the sheriff and Judge Kelly. I'd own the whole of Mustang County.'

Gault was watching him with cold, steel-blue eyes and a face like a marble mask. 'Shore—after Lane checks out. But he's only forty-five; he might live as long again.'

Ham shrugged. 'That's in the cards, of course; but with this war between homesteader and cattleman—' He left the rest unsaid, and for a moment there was a heavy silence.

'Wouldn't take much to start somethin' between the Woodwards and him,' said

Gault, at last. He flashed a knowing look at Turner. 'Maybe that's what yuh had in mind when yuh ordered me to shoot that cow and drag it across the boundary.'

'Perhaps it was,' admitted Ham. 'However, I made the mistake of not taking time to think the thing through, and you made a mistake in shooting an old cow instead of a yearling. That let Kirk Woodward wriggle out of the trap. There should be a better way. Suppose we think it over, eh?'

'There's lots of ways,' said Sarge slowly. 'The Woodwards have always pretended to be gosh-awful righteous about rustlin'; suppose a hide with a JKL brand was to be found on their land? That ought to start somethin'.'

'It would be a good beginning. But it must be done artistically—nothing crude or slipshod. I'll leave it to you. Meanwhile, I'll be a rather frequent visitor at the JKL ranch house and talk myself hoarse over poetry and art and literature.'

'Yuh're takin' a lot for granted, ain't yuh? Seems like I heard somethin' about this Kirk Woodward and the Lane girl bein' pretty sweet on each other before she went East.'

'You're probably thinking of the younger girl, Nellie. I know for a fact that Barbara hates Kirk Woodward like poison, and he insults her at every opportunity. In any event, he won't last long. I told him plainly that I intended to get him, and if we can't manage it

39

through the JKL we can call on Virg and Stoney. Virg had both guns on him last night and I wanted to give the word so badly that it hurt; but I had to check him or turn Barbara against me for life.'

'Thought she hated Woodward?'

'My dear fellow, women are squeamish about such things. They'll beg you to kill a snake and then turn their heads while you're about it ... Well, I guess that's all. If there's nothing else to discuss you can send Cliff in and I'll furnish him with money for his payroll.'

Gault got up. 'Just one more thing. You say this whole deal is between you and me. Where does Venner come in?'

'He doesn't. He's a very small cog in the machine. You and I stand together, nobody else. We'll figure on the sheriff's job for you to begin with. It's a big graft. After that—who knows?'

Gault turned and went out, satisfied. Ham leaned back in his chair and smiled benignly. He was well pleased with himself.

★   ★   ★

The fence on the Flying W had been repaired and the three men gathered about the supper table where Kirk and Tom acquainted their father with what had happened at the creek that morning. Asa Woodward was indignant at first, but presently anger gave way to concern.

'It looks bad, boys. We've shot JKL stock in the past when we found it on our side of the line, just as Lane shoots ours when they stray; but always we drag them to his range and leave them untouched. Somebody is tryin' to make it look as though we're rustlin'.'

'It would have to be either the M or some of the lot down at Bates' Bottom,' said Kirk. 'I don't see what object the M could have. They know they can get Lane's help against us for the askin'. And the boys in the Bottom would be the last to start Jonathan on a rustlin' clean-up.'

'I'll find out about Bates' Bottom,' promised Tom. 'I got me a few friends down there who'll wise me up if I go after them the right way.'

He left the room and presently Kirk heard him ride away. Asa Woodward busied himself with a stock journal and Kirk got up and went out. He saddled his horse and rode along the south fence to the creek. A heavy silence enveloped him as he lounged in his saddle looking down at the scene of the morning's encounter.

He lived again every moment of it. Thought of Ham's discomfiture when the tables were turned brought a grin. He saw again the two girls, Barbara stiff and uncompromising. Vivian Stacy with her dimpled cheeks and languorous eyes. 'I think you're splendid!' she had said. He chuckled aloud. 'She knew it was a cow!' he murmured. 'Old hoss, you heard her say it, and you seen how flabbergasted Barbara was. Lordy, what a girl!'

What a girl indeed! Rich, glamorous, used to luxury and ease, as far above as the stars. She an heiress; he, a poor nester. But suppose old Tanglefoot Tarberry made his strike! As his grubstaker Kirk would be entitled to half of what the old coot found; and if that ledge were anywhere as rich—

He pulled up with a chuckle for his foolishness and abruptly reined his horse towards home. But even as he dropped off to sleep, great chunks of virgin gold glittered before his eyes and he was dancing a fandango of glee with Tanglefoot Tarberry.

An hour or so later he awakened as Tom tiptoed into the room.

'Find out anything?' he whispered, so as not to disturb their father.

'No. Nobody there but a couple of cripples. Shab and the rest are below the line with those JKL cattle. Say, you didn't give that old fool Tanglefoot Tarberry any money, did you?'

Kirk sat up. 'Me? Why?'

'The danged old liar got hold of some somewhere. He's layin' in a corner drunk as a

42

hoot owl. Spent close to fifty bucks on booze and blackjack. I tell you, the next time he comes here for a handout—'

Kirk did not hear the rest. He sank back in his bunk and closed his eyes, and this time no glittering gold danced before them.

CHAPTER FOUR

There was activity on the M that night. A herd of several hundred choice steers, each wearing the Box V brand, was driven by Venner and Gault and the M cowboys through the pass in the Mustangs to the fenced areas supposedly owned by Cliff Venner.

C. Hamilton Turner did not accompany the drive. He was no cattleman, and his interest in dumb animals was limited to the monetary profit their sale would bring him in. Even on the back of a horse he was at a disadvantage; because of his handsome appearance and the neatness of his trappings he looked well while at rest, but once the animal was in motion all semblance of grace and efficiency ceased. Matters pertaining to the breeding and raising of stock he left to Gault. He had never learned to use a lariat, and carried a short-barreled, nickel-plated revolver which his cowboys eyed with amusement and scorn.

Although the Mustangs separated the two ranges as effectively as though they were in different states, the drive was not a long one. There was little need for caution, the chance of encountering anybody in the pass being remote. East- or westbound travelers took the more direct route which ran directly through the town.

When the drive got under way, Turner went into his office and for some time busied himself with plans for the future. When the crew returned they would be put to work gathering more prime Monarch steers, changing the M to a Box V, and turning them into the well-guarded southeast pasture for the reworked brands to heal. After that—well, there was plenty to do.

The various expedients he used to enrich himself at the expense of his employers were at once ingenious and simple. In addition to the appropriation of beef 'critters' he had a well-stocked breeding herd, all property of the M. A large percentage of the increase of this herd was immediately branded with the Box V and turned over to Venner, and since no question of alteration in the brand could arise, there was no danger of apprehension. Faked purchases of cattle and land, padded payrolls and expense accounts, had netted him thousands of dollars. For the Monarch was an immense spread and a man as clever as C. Hamilton Turner could dig quite deeply into its resources before his defalcation became apparent. This is especially true where the owners are two thousand miles away and at the mercy of their manager's discretion. In addition to all this there was the cut of the selling price of JKL cattle which he received from the inhabitants of Bates' Bottom for his help in pushing the rustled stuff across the line.

All in all, decided Turner, things were shaping up very nicely. The resourceful Gault would devise a means of throwing the Woodwards and the Lanes into open warfare, and regardless of the outcome Ham must profit. If the Woodwards were exterminated or driven out, he would take possession of their homestead as well as those to the north; if Lane ~~were~~ killed, the power he craved would be his. Also the mighty JKL, if affairs progressed as he confidently expected them to. In Ham's estimation Barbara, despite her Eastern education, was still a simple ranch girl, unsophisticated and easily dazzled. And as a dazzler, Ham considered himself without peer. It should be a simple matter to rush the girl off her feet and into his greedy arms. So at last Ham locked his books and papers in the safe and went to bed to sleep the untroubled sleep of the man who sees no clouds on the horizon, and if he dreamed, it was probably a dream of wealth and affluence in the days to come.

Down in Bates' Bottom, Tanglefoot Tarberry slept also, a deep, drunken slumber that was dreamless and profound. He lay in a corner of the dive owned by Rum Blossom Bates, and when Joe Tripp, the bartender, decided that it was time to close up, they carried Tanglefoot outside and deposited him on the ground where he would be out of the way.

He awoke with the sun in his face and the stamp of hoofs in his ears, and lay for a moment blinking. The sounds persisted and he finally struggled to an elbow. Horses were lined up at the watering trough outside the saloon, and on them sat the Bottom boys who had driven Lane's cows into Mexico. The success of their trip was attested by their good nature.

Tanglefoot's hands shook and his head throbbed and his body was full of aches from sleeping so long on the hard ground, but these pains were insignificant when compared with those of his conscience at remembrance of the squandered grubstake. Fifty precious dollars gone to the very last cent! Fifty dollars thrown away on blackjack and the vile stuff the Bottom boys called whiskey! And what had he to show for it? A head like a bass drum and an awful taste in his mouth! He groaned aloud in his misery, and getting to his feet, began stamping up and down to restore his circulation, meanwhile berating himself in terms which were both bitter and profane.

Rum Blossom Bates, on his way to the table, drew rein and spoke wonderingly. 'What in the blinkin' hell's eatin' yuh?'

Tanglefoot told him. He had been a danged old fool. There he was, with enough money to outfit him, money which would have enabled him to find that lost gold, and he had gone and tossed it away. Yes, sir; he just couldn't wait until he owned a million dollars to get drunk, he had to go and do it right away. And now here he was, starting from scratch again, broke and hungry and without a friend in the world to stake him to a new outfit.

Bates was not very sympathetic. 'Why don't yuh go out and rustle yoreself another grubstake?'

'Ain't nothin' I kin do,' whined Tanglefoot. 'I'm jest a old, throwed-away man and a humpbacked diddledy-dad-burned fool to boot. Who do yuh think would give me a job?'

'Nobody said nothin' about a job.' Rum Blossom waved a brawny arm. 'Over thar's the JKL, and down thar's Mexico. Rustle yoreself some cows an' run 'em over the line.'

Tanglefoot blinked at him. The idea was a bit startling. 'Ain't got no hoss or rig.'

'Thar's Jerry,' said Bates, nodding towards a bony old horse that was nibbling at the scant grass at the edge of the settlement. 'He

47

ain't no greased lightnin', but he's sound. And yuh oughta be able to make yoreself a rig from the stuff up in the barn loft.'

He rode on down to the stable and Tanglefoot stood there thinking hard. Jerry was all of twenty-five years old and had been turned out to die years before. He hung around the Bottom for the occasional handful of grain doled out by a patronizing outlaw. He would do in a pinch. But rustling! That was bad business—dangerous business. They hanged rustlers when they caught them. Tanglefoot put the idea from him only to snatch it back at thought of his desperate need. He had sworn to Kirk Woodward that this time he would use the money for the purpose it was given him; Kirk would skin him alive if he found out. He just had to get back somehow, and come to think of it, rustling from the JKL wasn't so bad after all. Wasn't Jonathan Lane the avowed enemy of his friend, Kirk? And also wasn't everybody and his brother helping themselves to Lane's cows? And it should be a comparatively easy job; all you had to do was drive the critters below the line. Why, even if he had to haze them off one at a time, half a dozen trips—

He shuffled down to the barn, climbed the ladder to the loft and began rooting amongst the discarded saddles, rusted bits and moldly leather straps. Tossing what he wanted to the ground, he descended, a new eagerness in his movements. He knew where Bates kept his harness-mending equipment. The rest of that day and the whole of the next he worked steadily, sleeping in the hay and bumming his meals from Pegleg Johnson and Pappy Bates, who had skinned him at blackjack. He considered that they owed him this much.

At sunset of the second day he coaxed the unsuspecting Jerry within reach of some grain stolen from Rum Blossom's feed shed. The makeshift saddle was cinched and tied in place, the homemade hackamore adjusted, and after several years of luxury and idleness the surprised Jerry found himself with a passenger.

Tanglefoot gave a shrill and rather trembly whoop and kicked his steed in the bony ribs. The oddly assorted pair started out on the highroad of Adventure!

At almost the same moment Sarge Gault and Ham Turner left the M. Both parties were bent on the same errand—the theft of a JKL steer—although their reasons for the stealing differed greatly. Ham was driving a buckboard, and Gault, astride his horse, trotted beside the vehicle.

'I wish you could have done without me,' complained Ham. He did not relish taking risks when he could hire men to take them for him.

Gault's answer was heavy with logic. 'This thing is too important to risk takin' another in with us, and I cain't handle it alone. We can use the crew in a simple thing like changin' an M to a Box V; every danged one's a rustler himself and in it as deep as the rest. But this thing of gettin' two fellers ripe to kill each other is ticklish business. If one of 'em gets wise, there'll be hell to pay. Take another man in and yuh'll have to explain why or let him guess. You and me are in this deal alone and that's the way we're gonna stay.'

'You're right, of course,' conceded Ham, and thereafter they rode in silence. Darkness gathered. The stars came out, bright and crinkly; there would be no moon until midnight. When they neared the Flying W they reined to a walk. Gault had greased the buckboard wheels and they made but little noise. Presently he gave the signal to halt and climbed down from his horse.

Leaving the reins dragging, he tied the buckboard to a tree, then took from the vehicle a singletree and block and tackle, and a short-handled sledge. These he fastened to his saddle, after which he mounted.

'Yuh'll have to walk,' he told Ham. 'Fetch the spade and keep close to my hoss. It ain't far. I looked over the ground today and picked the right spot for the job.'

He started for the creek bed to his left and Ham followed. They descended the bank to the dry bottom of the creek, followed it to where the overflow from the Flying W water hole entered it, then waded the stream to the Woodward range. Ascending the east bank, Gault guided his horse through the brush to an open spot beneath a small oak. Here he dismounted.

'No use gettin' panicky,' he said quietly. 'If anybody comes along just duck and lay low. They'll never see yuh in the dark. We'll take it right easy. Stay here while I get the steer.' He unfastened the tackle and singletree and sledge and placed them on the ground, then rode silently away.

Straight to the JKL range he rode, searching among the resting cattle for one which would suit his purpose. The animals rose at his approach and moved sluggishly out of his way. He circled, picked the one he wanted, and started hazing it towards the creek. The steer trotted off to the right and the wise cow horse headed it. To the left it bolted, only to be headed again. With an indignant snort, the animal descended the bank to the creek bed.

Gault's rope flicked out, circled the steer's horns. Leaving plenty of slack in the lariat, he urged his mount up the far bank, then literally dragged the balky steer up after him.

Ham came running up. 'For Heaven's sake be quiet!' he whispered hoarsely. 'You're making enough racket to raise the dead!'

'Cain't help it. Jest a bit farther.'

The animal was dragged to the oak. Gault

51

circled the tree, drew the steer's head against the trunk, dismounted and snubbed the animal there. Then for a full five minutes they stood listening. There was no sound save the heavy breathing and occasional protesting grunts of the steer.

'Keno,' said Gault at last. 'Where's that sledge?'

He dispatched the animal, slackened the rope and cut the steer's throat. The tackle was attached to a projecting limb, the steer's rear hocks were fastened to the singletree, and the carcass was raised until it swung clear. Expertly Gault severed the head and skinned it down. Picking up the spade, he led the way to a cleared spot in the midst of some heavy chaparral.

'Dig a hole deep enough for the head and hide,' he directed Turner. 'I'll be cuttin' it up while yuh're doin' it.'

He went to the hanging steer and Ham started digging. By the time he had finished, Sarge was back with hide and head. He tossed them into the hole.

'Cover 'em up good and smooth it off. Pile some brush atop it. Do it like yore life depended on not havin' anybody find it. I've left the feet and entrails, and by noon there ought to be plenty of buzzards.'

While Ham worked, Gault carried the meat back to the buckboard, where it was wrapped in gunny sacks. By the time he had finished,

Ham was through with his task. Sarge made a careful inspection of the whole job and pronounced himself satisfied. The entire thing had been executed without the slightest hitch.

'Let's go,' he said, and got on his horse. Ham followed in his tracks. Sweat was on Turner's brow and his muscles ached, but there was malicious satisfaction in his heart. The trap was baited and set!

★   ★   ★

Tanglefoot Tarberry, the rustler, was not doing so well. His equipment was inadequate and so was his mount. A stirrup broke before he had gone a mile, and at the same time Jerry took it into his head to settle into a rough trot that tossed Tanglefoot about like a bit of corn in the popper. He cursed the horse, but to no avail; he could only hang to the ancient horn with his left hand and try to steer Jerry with the right.

It was a long ride to the JKL range, and since Tanglefoot was no horseman he began to develop strange new pains in various parts of his anatomy. When Jerry finally tired of the trot, he settled into a sedate walk, pausing occasionally and unexpectedly to stab at a bunch of grass. At each thrust of his telescopic neck, Tanglefoot was nearly yanked over his head. At such times the exasperated old man would drum the ancient flanks with his spurless heels and slap Jerry on the rump with his dilapidated hat; but Jerry would eat calmly away until a desire for fresh pastures would stir him into his ambling walk once more. Tanglefoot sighed and wished earnestly for a club, but was afraid to dismount and hunt for one for fear that his steed would desert him.

When he reached the JKL range he thought his troubles were over for the moment. Jerry became unusually placid, moving sluggishly among the cattle while Tanglefoot peered through the darkness trying to select a steer that looked easy to drive. As it turned out, he might better have taken his chance of finding a club, for Jerry's ambling walk grew steadily slower and at last, with a heavy sigh, he lay down.

Tanglefoot stepped off and looked down at him with an expression of profound disgust. 'Yuh danged old quitter, mebbe yuh want me to carry you! Wal, yuh can lay there and turn to fertilizer fer all I care! Sound, Rum Blossom said yuh were. Huh! If yuh're sound I'm that there Samson feller with the long hair! Yuh ain't tuckered out; yuh're jest plumb lazy. If I had a club—'

He broke off to look about him in the hope of finding such an implement, and the next moment was flat on the ground beside the horse. Against the skyline not a hundred yards away he had seen a rider—a rider who moved slowly, ghostlike, along the crest of a ridge.

Tanglefoot's first thought was that it was a JKL rider on the prowl, and he had a fleeting vision of himself dangling at the end of a long rope; then he decided that it was one of the Bottom boys picking up a little revenue and lost his fear in a curiosity as to how the fellow went about it. Rustling, concluded Tanglefoot, was something about which he had a lot to learn. He started towards the rider, moving quietly, crouched close to the ground.

The horseman disappeared below the crest, and Tanglefoot hurried to a point where he could see him. And now he noticed that the rider was hazing a steer before him, slowly but inexorably towards the bank of the creek. Old Tanglefoot nodded understandingly and followed. He was learning.

On the bank of the creek he waited and watched while the other roped the critter and dragged it up the far bank. Something told him that this was not as it should be. By rights the fellow should be driving the animal down the creek bed instead of taking him on the Flying W. Then he thought that the rustler might be Kirk Woodward. But Kirk's antipathy to rustling was well known. Maybe it was Tom!

He slid down the bank and ascended the

far side, the noise of his progress drowned by the sound of man and animals. Then he heard a frantic admonition to be quiet, and the terse answer, 'Cain't help it. Jest a bit further.' The voices were lowered and he did not recognize them.

Tanglefoot bedded down behind some bushes and listened with both ears. He heard the creak of tackle, whispered instructions. Then his heart nearly stopped as two vague figures came directly towards him. To his relief, they stopped some twenty feet away and one of them started to dig.

Tanglefoot lay there, hardly daring to breathe. The digger worked steadily, the other made several trips to the Monarch range and back; and finally he heard a gruff, 'Let's go,' and immediately thereafter a horseman rode towards the M with the second man following on foot. Then Tanglefoot heard the distant rattle of wheels and the thud of hoofs, and knew that he was safe from discovery.

Getting up, he went to the place where the man had been digging, removed the brush and started scooping away the loose dirt with his hands. He felt damp air, and quickly identified what had been buried. Stopping abruptly, he settled back on his haunches and for one reputed to be but half-witted his brain was working inordinately fast.

'Wal, the *dirty—low*down—*thievin'—hump*backed—*degen'*rates!' he swore.

He wasn't sure what a degenerate was, but at the moment the word seemed eminently fitting. He thought hard for a few moments, then set to work.

CHAPTER FIVE

Barbara Lane and C. Hamilton Turner rode slowly along the road which led to the Flying W. Barbara talked animatedly, and Ham tried hard to concentrate on what she was saying, but despite his best efforts his attention wandered and his eyes kept searching the sky. He was watching three dots that circled slowly above the Woodward homestead. As they drew nearer the creek the dots began circling downward, growing in size, and presently Barbara, catching his glance, looked up, too.'

'Buzzards,' she remarked. 'Graceful, but ugly.'

'And necessary,' he added. 'They keep the range clean. I wonder what has attracted them?' They watched as the birds settled lower and lower, finally disappearing beyond the trees. 'Whatever it is is on the Woodward spread. Shall we have a look?'

She nodded and they put spurs to their horses. Fording the creek, they ascended the far bank and forced their mounts through the

57

brakes, and suddenly there came a lazy flapping of wings as the scavengers rose from the ground. The riders halted.

'Somebody has butchered a steer,' announced Barbara.

'Peculiar place to do it,' said Ham. 'If it was a Flying W animal why didn't they dress it in their killing pen? It looks suspicious to me; I think your father should be told about it.'

They rode swiftly to the JKL headquarters. Lane was talking with Sarge Gault, who had accompanied Ham in order to be on hand at the climax. Turner reported briefly. 'Thought you might want to take a look,' he concluded.

'I shore do,' said Lane, and started for the corral, calling to half a dozen of his cowboys to saddle up and accompany him. Gault and Ham went along, but Barbara remained behind.

They crossed to the Woodward range cautiously, alert for trouble, but nobody appeared to oppose them. Again the wings flapped and the buzzards rose reluctantly from their feast. Lane looked about carefully, framing the details of the butchering in his mind.

'Only one way of findin' out,' he said at last. 'If it was one of their own critters they'd keep the head and the hide. We'll ride up to the house and look around.'

They emerged from the brakes to the

Woodward range and loped across it, momentarily expecting to be challenged, but the buildings they approached were quite evidently deserted. Lane hailed as a matter of precaution, received no answer, and kicked open the door. For the better part of an hour they painstakingly searched house and outbuildings without finding a fresh hide or any signs of newly butchered meat, and finally Lane called them together.

Ham Turner spoke. 'An animal was most certainly butchered, and it stands to reason that it was a Flying W or a JKL one. If it was yours, Jonathan, they probably buried the head and hide so there would be no earmarks or brand to give them away.'

'We'll ride back to the place and look,' said Lane.

Back at the scene of the killing they began a systematic search. And then they froze as a sharp voice challenged them and they looked up to see Tom Woodward sitting his horse with his rifle leveled at them. The dense brush had prevented their noticing his approach.

'What's goin' on here?' he demanded harshly.

Lane answered. 'There's plenty goin' on, my young buck. You better drop that rifle, for we're ten to yore one and we're in no mood for foolishness.'

Tom's eyes were blazing and he still held

the rifle rigidly. 'You're trespassin', every danged one of you, and I am to learn why.'

'You will.' Lane pointed to the remains of the butchered steer. 'A JKL or a Monarch steer was butchered here and we aim to find out which it was. We're lookin' for the head and the hide.'

Tom glanced in the direction indicated and when he looked back he found himself covered by several rifles.

'You accusin' us of beefin' yore steers?' he demanded angrily.

'I'm accusin' you of nothin'—yet. When we found this stuff I figured it might have been a Flyn' W critter. We went to the house and found nobody there, so we made free to look around. There was no hide, no head, and no fresh meat.'

'Then how do you figure that we butchered a steer?'

'I don't reckon you'd keep it lyin' around where anybody could find it. Now drop that rifle before we drop you.'

'You're danged right I'll drop it!' cried Tom, and flung it from him. But the next moment he was on the ground and advancing towards Lane. 'If you want to shoot an unarmed man, hop to it! But nobody calls a Woodward a thief and gets away it!'

He leaped at Lane and the JKL owner braced himself to meet the attack. Tom closed like a puma, savagely, swiftly; but

Jonathan Lane was a big man and had fought more formidable enemies than Tom Woodward. Calling to his men to keep hands off, he lunged forward to meet the boy, his heavy fists flailing.

Some of Tom's blows landed and when they did they stung; but Lane only grunted and swung the harder, and presently one of his haymakers caught Tom on the temple and sent him spinning. As the boy lay dazed, Lane indicated Sarge Gault, who stood nearest him.

'Watch him. The rest of you get to work huntin' for that hide.'

They resumed the search, ranging back and forth, and suddenly Ham Turner cried out triumphantly. 'Here's some leaves with blood on them, Jonathan!'

Lane went over quickly, glanced about him and got his bearings from the tree in which the steer had been hung and walked slowly towards a pile of brush. Then he stopped and called to a cowboy. 'Move that brush and see what's under it.' When it was done, he exclaimed his satisfaction. 'I thought so! New packed earth. Scoop it away, Slim. Help him, Tex.'

The two cowboys shoveled away the loose dirt with their hands while Ham watched eagerly; but to his consternation nothing was revealed.

'Deeper!' he cried. 'Dig deeper. It must be

there.'

But it wasn't. The cowboys removed every bit of loose dirt until it became apparent that no farther progress could be made without a shovel.

Lane turned fiercely to Tom. The boy had got to his feet and stood shaking with weakness and rage under the cocked gun of Sarge Gault. 'You danged foxes! That hide was hid here last night when the steer was beefed. One of you Woodwards moved it since!'

'That's a lie! The three of us rode out in the hills before it was light to haze strays out of the timber. My hoss went lame and I came back for another one. When I came out of the woods I saw you and followed. You danged fool! If we took the trouble to bury the head and the hide, why didn't we bury the entrails too, instead of leavin' them here to draw all the buzzards in the country?'

It was a question which Lane had not asked himself, and the answer was not easy to find. He turned away and spoke harshly. 'Get busy, all of you, and find that hide! By Godfrey, it's got to be somewhere!'

But search as they would they could not locate it, and finally Lane made a gesture of futility and called them together.

'It's no use,' he said, looking angrily at Tom. 'They've outfoxed us again. As long as we cain't prove it was a stolen steer we can do nothin'. But I'm warnin' you, Woodward, and you can pass this along to yore father and brother: I'll be watchin' you close from here on, and if I ever catch any one of you monkeyin' with my stock I'll plug him as shore as I live!'

'And now let me tell *you* somethin'!' cried Tom. 'I aim to stick around here the rest of the day, and from now on one of us will be watchin' our boundary all the time; and if I ever catch a JKL man on our land I'll shoot him down without even givin' him a chance to tell me why he's here! Now get out, all of you, and stay out!'

For another few seconds the boy and Lane stood glaring at each other, then the latter, with a brief gesture, turned to his horse. As Gault holstered his gun, Tom spoke to him. 'And that goes for you, too, Gault, and that sissy-faced boss of yores. Stay off the Flyin' W or be greeted with a lead kiss!'

When they had crossed to the road, Ham Turner motioned to Gault and turned his horse towards the M. The two men rode in silence until they were out of earshot, then Ham spoke to his foreman, his voice harsh with anger and disappointment. 'What in hell happened this time?'

'Yuh got me—unless one of the Woodwards found and moved them.'

'Then why did they leave those entrails?'

It was an unanswerable question, and they

lapsed again into silence. Finally Gault spoke again.

'Come to think of it, things ain't pannin' out bad as they are. We started somethin' between Lane and the Woodwards—a shooting war. If Lane ever sets foot on the Flyin' W range, Tom'll shoot him shore as hell.'

Ham flashed him a searching look. 'Hm-m-m,' he said. 'That's something to think about, isn't it?'

By the time Lane reached the JKL ranch house he had cooled down somewhat. He still believed sincerely that the Woodwards had slaughtered a JKL steer and had concealed the hide, head, and meat, but he was still seeking the answer to Tom's question. If they had taken such great pains to dispose of the rest of the steer, why had they left entrails and feet uncovered?

He could not leave the puzzle unsolved, and after eating a hurried dinner, set out all alone, determined to find that missing head and hide if such a thing were possible. As he rode past the Flying W he heard a stir on the opposite creek bank and saw young Tom Woodward grimly watching him, his rifle ready to swing into line. Lane jerked his head forward and stuck to his side of the boundary.

He emerged on the road which led to the M and rode slowly along it, his gaze searching the brush on both sides of the trail. And presently there came again that heavy flapping of wings, and a buzzard rose from a patch of chaparral on his left. He reined the horse through the brush and found what he was looking for within twenty feet of the road.

It was a JKL steer that had been slaughtered; the earmarks were plainly discernible from the saddle and he could even see the L and part of the K on the hide.

Lane involuntarily glanced back towards the Flying W. He was not over a hundred yards from the boundary, and it seemed very evident that the Woodwards had carried the head and hide here to divert suspicion from themselves. He rode back to the dusty trail and looked for footprints. There they were, plain enough for anybody to see. He leaned from the saddle and examined them carefully. The boots which had made them were sadly worn; there was a gaping hole in one sole and both heels were worn down clear to the uppers. They were not cowboy boots, but flat-heeled ones such as prospectors and miners wore. Another dodge to throw him off the trail?

He urged his horse back along the road, scanning the tracks closely. And then he became aware of something else: The wagon tracks which he had noticed without paying them any particular attention ended abruptly at the Flying W line. It was easy to see where the vehicle had been turned, and there, under a stunted tree, the team had been tied for a short while. Then Lane exclaimed in amazement and dropped from his horse. There were some dark spots in the road and he recognized them for drops of blood!

Grimly he ranged back and forth, reading the story written in the dirt. He found other blood spots at intervals between the first one and the Woodward boundary, but there were none beyond the point where the wagon had been turned; therefore they could not have been made by the hide or head. Those dark spots had been made by blood from the butchered meat, and that meat had been hauled away in the wagon. It began to look as though the Woodwards were innocent after all!

Jonathan mounted and followed the wagon tracks. They must lead him to one of two places: the Monarch ranch house or Bates' Bottom. He was sure it would be the latter, but when he reached the fork in the road which bore east towards the Bottom he was amazed to see that the tracks continued in the direction of the M. The knowledge floored him for a minute; then he remembered several significant facts and his face hardened.

Ham Turner had discovered the buzzards in the sky; Ham had gone directly to the spot where the steer had been butchered; Ham had found the spot of blood which betrayed the place where hide and head had been buried!

Lane saw a great light. Just south of the Monarch lay Mexico; might not the case-hardened crew of the M be guilty of the rustling which was stripping him of stock? Just how heavy his losses had been would not be determined until round-up, but they were undoubtedly great. Was Ham Turner at the bottom of the thefts?

Turner and Gault were seated on the M ranch-house gallery when Jonathan rode into the yard, and so grim was his aspect that they both got up and went to meet him. He sat his big horse, looking down at them gravely.

'You've discovered something?' inquired Ham.

'I have. I found the head and hide in the brush this side of the Flyin' W line. It was on Monarch property.'

Ham's surprise was real enough. 'Somebody certainly had a nerve!'

'And also,' continued Lane implacably, 'I found signs which told me that the meat of that steer was hauled back here to the M in a wagon. Turner, I'm askin' yore permission to make a search for it.'

'That I can never grant,' said Ham firmly. 'I'm surprised and a bit pained to think that you should ask it.'

'I haven't accused you of havin' anything to

do with it, but yore refusal to let me search is suspicious. I'm in no position to insist, and if that meat is on this spread you'd have it moved by the time I could ride after my boys. I'm not makin' an issue of that one steer, but from now on I'll have my eyes peeled. I don't reckon anybody is goin' to pull the wool over them again. And now I'm ridin' straight to the Flyin' W and apologize to Tom Woodward; and I'll do it from my knees if he wants it thataway.'

He wheeled his horse and rode away, his straight, broad back to them. Gault half drew his gun but Ham's hand gripped his arm, and the M manager whispered a terse, 'Wait!' When Lane swung around the corrals and disappeared from view, he turned to Gault and spoke swiftly.

'He's going over on the Flyin' W! Sarge, it's our chance! If Tom don't kill him—!'

Gault nodded. 'Get yore hoss. We can circle to the east and beat him there.'

In a matter of minutes only they were speeding from the ranch. They did not go by the road, but circled eastward towards the pass, then cut across the range to the trees which lined the small stream running from the Flying W water hole and extending westward. Presently they halted and got off their horses. Listening, they could hear the drum of hoofs on the road. Each had a rifle; on the face of each was a look of grim resolve.

Lane must not be permitted to reveal his findings to Tom. They crossed the little stream and climbed its far bank until they could see over its top. There was a double click as the rifles were cocked.

Jonathan Lane splashed his horse through the stream and urged him up the bank to the Woodward homestead. His rifle was in its boot and both hands were held above his head as he knee-rode his horse out on the open range.

A hundred yards before him Tom Woodward sat waiting, his rifle at his shoulder, but Lane did not falter. Slowly the horse moved forward, its rider's hands still in the air.

'Stop where you are!' cried Tom, and Jonathan obediently halted. 'I swore I'd kill you if you set foot on our land, but I cain't shoot a man who got his hands up. What do you want?'

'I wouldn't blame you if you had shot me, son,' said Lane quietly. 'But I had to take the chance. I've done you a big wrong, boy, and I've come to apologize.'

Tom lowered the rifle. 'Apologize? You found out who done it?'

'Yeah, I found out who done it. It knocked me silly. I found—'

Tom saw him jerk in the saddle, saw the dust fly from his vest directly over his heart. The whipcrack of a rifle came from behind him and to his left. Lane sat for a moment perfectly still, his hands still raised, but a spasm of pain contorted his face and his eyes were staring. Then the horse made a little nervous movement and Lane toppled from the saddle like a wet sack.

'My God!' cried Tom hoarsely, and reined his mount. The quick movement saved him, for again came that vicious crack and lead bored the air where a moment before his head had been.

Tom dived from the saddle into the tall grass and raised his Winchester. A tiny puff of smoke ascended from the bank of the creek a hundred and fifty yards away. He fired quickly, fiercely, again and again; but there was no target and his lead merely cut through the leaves of the trees.

He watched like a hawk, searching the bank for movement, but in vain. Presently he raised his hat above the top of the grass. There was no shot and he got up and ran quickly to Jonathan's side. Feverishly he felt the man's pulse, held his cheek close to the opened mouth. There was no doubt of it: Jonathan Lane was dead!

Back to his horse he sped, to ride him headlong towards the place from whence the shot had come. His jaws were tightly set and the rifle was ready. He found nothing. On the bank of the stream he discovered where two horses had been briefly tied. But there was nothing whatever to identify horses or riders. Grass does not leave a plain trail.

Worriedly he recrossed the stream and started up the bank. A shout reached him, a shout of consternation and rage. He checked the horse, flung himself from the saddle, crept to the top of the bank and peered over.

A group of men had gathered in a little circle about the prostrate Lane, and he recognized them for JKL cowboys. Hastily he clambered down the bank and mounted his horse; quietly he re-forded the stream and worked his way through the trees on its far side. His brow was moist with perspiration and his eyes were wide like those of a frightened child.

He couldn't go back there and tell them how it had happened. He had publicly threatened to kill Lane if he stepped on Woodward land, and now Lane was lying there—dead! There were no witnesses, and nobody would believe his story. The cards were stacked against him. He dropped his head and a dry sob choked him. Face bleak with the tragedy of the thing, he turned his horse towards Bates' Bottom.

CHAPTER SIX

'Wonder what's become of Tom?' Kirk put the question to his father as they prepared to ride home. It had been close to noon when the younger Woodward had left them with the intention of getting another horse, and since each was covering a different sector they had assumed that he had returned to work.

'I shore don't know,' answered Asa Woodward worriedly. 'Thought he'd be right back. Yuh reckon somethin' happened to him?'

'I heard two rifle shots a short while ago, but didn't pay much attention. They sounded far off—down by the creek or over on the JKL.'

'Well, he ain't in the hills, or he'd be here by now. We better drive down what we have.'

The cattle they had hazed out of the hills on their last circle were started down the wooded slope towards the open range, and as they followed the two men talked.

'Kirk, I been thinkin' a heap about that dead cow Lane found on our spread. Who yuh reckon shot it and dragged it there?'

Kirk spoke slowly. 'Wasn't the Bottom boys; Tom told me they were all over the line except a few cripples. There's nobody on the JKL who'd do it just for the sake of makin' trouble, and we know none of the homesteaders want open war with Lane. That leaves only the Monarch.'

'Why would they do it? Yuh said yourself that Ham Turner could get Lane's help any time he wanted it. I just cain't figger it out.'

'Ham Turner's a mighty foxy gent. He's too danged ambitious to be workin' for the Monarch alone. He's gettin' a big rake-off on every deal he swings, I'll bet you money. Some day I'm goin' to take a trip to the county seat and see where title to these homesteads he bought or stole lies. If he recorded them in his own name we'll know he's crooked; and if he's crooked I can think of several reasons why he'd want us at war with Lane.'

'I'd like to hear one of 'em.'

'Well, if he's tryin' to get our place for himself, the less the Syndicate knows about it the better for Ham; so if he can maneuver the JKL into doin' his fightin' for him he can stand back and wait until Lane has us licked, then step in and take our place without any fuss. Lane don't want the Flyin' W, but he would like to see all nesters pushed out of the valley.'

'Got any more ideas?'

'Yes. Barbara just got back from the East and Ham has taken her eye. She's full of Eastern notions as a brush cow is of ticks and us fellers out here must look mighty rough and crude beside him. She'd be a rich catch for Ham and likely he realizes it. But he must have heard that Barbara and I were good friends once and he may be afraid of hurtin' his chances with her if he tries to clean us out by the Winchester route. That's just a hunch,' he went on quickly, 'and may be 'way off the mark.'

'I don't know what to think,' said Asa gloomily. 'I ain't used to this underhand business. I can understand a man's goin' openly after what he wants, and even if he's in the wrong I can respect him for the way he fights; but this shootin' of cows and draggin' 'em on another man's spread to make trouble between him and his neighbor is lowdown and dirty and I jest cain't figger one who'd be mean enough to do it.'

'Ham Turner could be equal to it. An education is a mighty good thing if it's rightly used, but a bad man with brains can do a lot of dirt.'

They turned the cattle loose on the open range and loped their horses towards the house. It was late afternoon when they drew up at the corral to discover immediately that the place was far from being deserted.

'Get yore hands up and keep them up!' came a sharp order, and both men froze in the saddle. Rifles covered them from behind the watering trough, the corners of the cabin and the outbuildings. Slim Chance stepped into sight, his Winchester held waist-high. Slim and Kirk had been friends once, but now the JKL foreman's eyes were cold with dislike.

'What's the matter, Slim?' asked Kirk. 'Some more dead cows?'

Slim ignored the sarcasm. 'Where's Tom?'

'That's more than I can tell you. He was with us helpin' haze cows out of the hills, but his hoss went lame and he came in for another. We haven't seen him since. What you want with him?'

'We want him for murder!' snapped Chance. 'He killed Jonathan Lane—shot him dead.'

Kirk and his father stared. 'No!' cried the former unbelievingly. 'Slim, what are you sayin'?'

'You heard me.' Slim cursed Tom bitterly. 'He had a run-in with Jonathan—warned him off the Flyin' W. Swore he'd shoot without warnin' any JKL man that set foot on this range. An hour ago we found Jonathan on yore side of the line, shot through the heart. If you were in the hills like you say, Tom did it as shore as hell!'

More men stepped into sight, and Kirk recognized them as JKL cowboys. Ordinarily they were a good-natured bunch, but now their faces were grim and they were in a lynching mood.

'Slim, what you've told us—well, I just cain't figure it. Tom's hot-headed and rash, but he's no cold-blooded killer. I've always known you for a square-shooter, and now it's time to spread yore cards. I reckon we're entitled to know the whole story.'

Slim told them, tersely and bitterly. 'We all know that steer yuh slaughtered was a JKL or an M critter, and we know that one of yuh moved the head and hide and hid the meat so's we couldn't find any proof. And because the whole deal was so plain, Jonathan got mad and told Tom that if he ever caught one of yuh monkeyin' with a JKL animal he'd shoot him in his tracks. Tom promised Jonathan that if a JKL man set foot on the Flyin' W he'd do the same.

'After dinner Jonathan rode towards the Flyin' W alone. When he didn't come back, Barbara got worried and sent us to look for him. We were nearin' the creek when we heard two rifle shots, close together. We rode over and found Jonathan dead. There ain't any doubt as to who did it. Jonathan had knocked Tom down and the boy was fightin' mad. We found where his hoss stood when he killed Lane. It wasn't more than fifty yards from where Lane lay.'

'My God!' groaned Asa Woodward.

'Slim,' said Kirk tightly, 'there's one thing I want to set you right on here and now. No steer, bull or cow, Flyin' W, JKL, or M, was slaughtered down there by the creek by any of the Woodwards. Godfrey, man! cain't you see that it's just the old dead cow trick carried a bit farther? As for those rifle shots, I heard them myself and told Dad they sounded as though they came from the creek; but the very fact that *two* shots were fired means that both men fired, in which case if Tom killed Jonathan he did it in self-defense.'

'Not much, he didn't! Jonathan's rifle was in the boot and his six-gun hadn't been touched. Neither of them had been fired. Kirk, if we find Tom, it's goin' to go hard with him. Jonathan Lane was our boss and there never was a better. But we aim to be fair about this thing. For the time bein' I'm takin' yore word that you and yore father had no part in the thing. We want Tom, and the harder to find him it is, the more certain we'll be that he did it.' He turned to his crew. 'Come on, boys, we'll search this range from one end to the other.'

They got their horses from the places where they had concealed them and rode away. Kirk watched dully. All good boys, these: Slim Chance, Tex Evans, Eaglebeak Smitty, Joe Calder, Sam and Chuck Brady—the rest of them. Some had worked for the JKL as long as Kirk could remember. Likable and easy-going they might be, but there was no question of their loyalty to Lane or of their intention to avenge his murder. Jonathan's killer would find no mercy at their hands.

'I just cain't believe it,' Kirk told his father. 'Somethin's happened that we know nothin' about. Those two shots—Tom was an expert with the rifle; he wouldn't have to shoot twice to hit a man once. Not at fifty yards, like Slim claims.'

'Might have fired one shot as a warnin',' suggested Asa dully.

'If Jonathan had warnin' he would have been carryin' his rifle or six-gun. You go in and get some supper; I'm goin' to have a look at those tracks while it's light enough to see.'

He rode to where Slim had told him the shooting took place. There were any number of tracks made by the JKL boys and cattle, but he easily found where Jonathan's big gelding had halted, and some fifty yards from these prints were marks which he recognized as having been made by Tom's second-string horse. On the face of it there appeared to be no doubt that Tom had shot Lane. Sick at heart, Kirk followed the faint trail which led towards the waterhole. Beyond the overflow stream he lost it, but there was no question in his mind as to where Tom had fled. He struck out for Bates' Bottom.

It was dusk by the time his horse had threaded the twisting trail which led to the hollow, and he found that others had preceded him. When he reached Bates' saloon it was to find Sheriff Jake Benson and a posse in charge. In pairs or threes they were going through shack and dive and investigating every possible hiding place. At another time the lawless inhabitants would have resisted with force of arms the liberties the sheriff was taking; but now most of them had withdrawn from the settlement rather than risk an encounter with Benson in his present savage mood.

Kirk entered the saloon just as Jake and his deputy, Skinny Stapleton, finished searching the storeroom, where a man could hide among the kegs and boxes. Skinny was fat and good-natured and lazy, but a holy terror when aroused, which is why Benson had selected him as his deputy. They had found no sign of Tom, and Jake, hard-faced and angry, spoke sharply to Woodward.

'So yuh figgered he'd head for here too, huh? Wal, if we uncover him—and we will if he's here—I'm warnin' yuh to keep out of it. Yuh try to interfere and there'll be another Woodward outa circulation ... Bates, what's that yuh're standin' on—a trapdoor?'

Rum Blossom looked down as though he had never seen it before. 'Why, danged if it ain't! Now how do yuh reckon that got there?'

'I wonder! Get off it and mebbe I can show yuh what it's used for.'

'Aw, they ain't nothin' down thar that yuh'd be interested in.'

'No? Get outa the way.' Benson pushed

79

him aside and drew his gun. Motioning Skinny to station himself on the opposite side, Jake got to his knees and slowly raised the trapdoor. The deputy trained his gun on the opening.

'Yuh might as well come up, Tom!' called the sheriff.

There was no answer. Benson laid the trapdoor to one side and peered into the pit, but the light failed to penetrate more than a few inches. Benson was no coward; he stretched out on the floor, struck a match and thrust the flame into the hole as far as he could reach. Then he jerked back the arm and bounded to his feet so suddenly that Skinny almost let the gun hammer slip from under his taut thumb.

'Holy bobcats! Why didn't you tell me there was a skunk down there?'

'Yuh didn't ask me,' replied Bates imperturbably. 'That's Annabelle. I dug that hole to make me a drain for the bar, and next time I looked Annabelle had moved in with her hull family. She was so doggoned cute I jest didn't have the heart to smoke her out. Allus liked the name Annabelle, which is why I give it to her. She won't hurt yuh—if yuh keep far enough away.'

'Wal, the polecat we're huntin' ain't named Annabelle,' said Jake savagely. 'Come on, Skinny. He ain't in here, that's shore.'

They left, and Kirk dropped a coin on the

bar.

'I'm lookin' for somethin', too. Got any idea where I can find it?'

Bates did not even look at him. 'Nary idea, Kirk. What yuh drinkin'?'

Kirk downed the harsh liquor and turned away. He was sure that somebody in the Bottom could give him news of Tom, but there was no chance of getting it while the posse was about. He rode back rapidly, but instead of stopping at the Flying W continued along the road which led to Mustang. An hour later he dropped off his horse before the JKL ranch house and rapped the door. Vivian opened it, started at sight of him, then moved to one side that he might enter.

Kirk stepped into the room. Barbara was there, and Ham Turner. The latter saw him first, and crossing the floor quickly, spoke harshly. 'You have gall coming here, Woodward!'

At sound of the name Barbara sprang to her feet. She had been crying, but now her grief was forgotten in revulsion at his presence.

Kirk, ignoring Turner, spoke gently to the girl. 'I rode over to tell you how sorry we are, Barbara.'

She stood stiff and straight before him, her hands clenched at her sides. 'I don't want your sympathy, Kirk Woodward! Your coming here is an insult to father's memory.

You—the brother of his murderer!'

'I cain't believe Tom's a murderer, Barbara; but leavin' that out of it, I speak for Father and me. We like to remember when yore family and ours were friends, as neighbors should be. Jonathan Lane was a good man and in spite of our differences we liked him. That's why I came over.'

Ham Turner spoke. 'I think you had better leave at once. Barbara is upset sufficiently as it is. If there was a reasonable doubt of Tom's guilt it might be different, but it's very plain that he killed Jonathan Lane and killed him without even giving him a chance to draw his gun. Get out, Woodward, or I'll summon the crew to put you out.'

Kirk did not answer him; to argue the point was entirely out of order at this time. He spoke again to Barbara. 'I meant what I said, Barbara, and if there is anything at all that we can do—'

'The only thing that you can do is leave,' she answered tightly. 'You must know how I feel towards you Woodwards. Tom will hang, and I intend to punish the rest of you as cruelly as I can. I will use every means at my command to drive you from Mustang range. I hate you! Hate you—all!' She sank into her chair, sobbing, and Kirk turned away. He had a glimpse of Nellie, white-faced and silent, busy with some task in the dining room. Vivian opened the door for him and followed him outside. He would have walked directly away but she put a hand on his arm and detained him.

'Barbara isn't herself, of course,' she said quietly. 'And Ham Turner isn't exactly helpful. We're all terribly upset and you mustn't be too harsh in your judgment of her.'

'I'm not even trying to judge her,' he said soberly. 'I knew I wouldn't be welcome, but I just had to come over. Honestly, Miss Stacy, I cain't believe that Tom killed Jonathan without givin' him a chance to defend himself.'

'I cain't either,' she said earnestly. 'I don't know Tom, but Nellie speaks of him as a big, reckless, laughing boy. Such a person could never be a wanton murderer.'

Kirk grasped her hand and pressed it tightly between his own. This was an entirely different Vivian Stacy from the one he had previously known.

'Thank you!' he murmured, and choked a bit as he said it.

He went quickly to his horse and mounted, but as he was about to rein away a figure stepped out of the shadows and the voice of Slim Chance came to him. 'I wouldn't ride over this way again, Kirk. The boys are all stirred up about this thing and yuh'll just be askin' for trouble. If yuh have to go to Mustang yuh can use the upper road.'

Again Kirk said nothing, but his cheeks were white with anger and humiliation as he rode away. And yet he could not blame them. He tried to imagine how he would feel if his father had been found dead on the JKL.

Asa Woodward was seated in a chair gazing moodily at the fire when Kirk reached the Flying W. His father nodded at some food on the stove.

'Better eat somethin'. We still got to keep the place goin'.'

Kirk swallowed the food without tasting it, then washed up the dishes and got wood and water for morning. They went to bed early and lay for a long while in their bunks, worried and sleepless. It would be all-out war from now on, war to the bitter end. Heretofore the JKL had remained aloof, giving moral support only to the efforts of the M to oust the Woodwards; now the homesteaders would have both outfits to fight. Kirk finally dozed.

He was awakened some hours later by his father, and as he opened his eyes he was immediately aware of a glow which streamed through the windows and illuminated the room. He sprang from his bunk and ran to the door. As he yanked it open a bullet smacked into the frame close to his head and he heard the sharp report of a rifle. It was plainly intended as a warning to stay inside. He closed the door and barred it, his face suddenly grim. Snatching up his rifle, he went to a window.

The barn was ablaze and a haystack beside it shot long tongues of flame into the air. Moving about just outside the circle of light were a dozen or more horsemen. One of them was in the act of opening the gate of the corral to release the frenzied animals within. Kirk raised his rifle to knock out a pane, but his father gripped his arm.

'No, son! No fightin' back this time. I reckon they figger we have it comin'.'

Kirk lowered the rifle and the two men stood side by side looking through the window. The JKL men were riding about restlessly, eyes on the cabin, rifles held ready to repulse any attempt of the Woodwards to fight the flames.

The roof of the barn caved in and an eruption of sparks and flame reached high, lighting the surroundings like a midday sun. Under the glare they both saw Barbara Lane. Slim and erect she sat her horse, her face hard, her eyes pitiless. Her hat hung by its throat latch and her dark hair fell in curls about her shoulders. Peculiarly Kirk was reminded of an old print of Sir Galahad he had once seen.

Ham Turner rode into the light and spoke to her, evidently urging her to withdraw. She waved him aside impatiently, and after an apprehensive glance towards the cabin he backed his horse into the shadows; but she remained while the flames leaped higher, reached their zenith and began to die. The JKL cowboys gathered in a bunch and Slim Chance rode up to her and spoke quietly, then motioned to his men and started off at a walk. One by one they followed until only she remained.

For another ten seconds she sat there, her form but a vague outline now; then she turned and was swallowed by the shadows, and for many days to come Kirk was to remember her small white face with tragedy written upon it.

Asa Woodward's hand fell on his son's shoulder. 'I reckon it's God's judgment, boy. We'll go out now and see what we can save.'

CHAPTER SEVEN

There was little they could do until the ashes were cold enough to permit them to clear away the wreckage. There would be no repairing to do, for the flames had taken everything they had touched.

Fire had visited Mustang range before this. The torch was the favorite weapon of the cattlemen against nesters, and while the Woodward place had been spared, they had seen the homes of their neighbors to the south of them go up in smoke under the attacks of the Monarch crew. Fire was a simple and effective weapon. Buildings and corrals cost money and labor to build, and if stock were consumed with them the loss was all the more keenly felt. The average homesteader was not a rich man by any means, and the destruction of his property was often more crippling than physical wounds.

Within the hour others from the homesteads to the north of them began to arrive, attracted by the glow in the sky. They came on horseback and in wagons, the latter carrying crude fire-fighting equipment. With their help the last smoldering embers were extinguished; then, gathering them about him, Kirk related the story of Jonathan Lane's death as reported by Slim.

It was plain to him, that most of them accepted Tom's guilt as a matter of fact, but being common enemies of the cattleman, openly upheld the boy.

'If Tom warned Jonathan off the Flyin' W and Jonathan refused to heed that warnin', the boy did the only thing he could do,' declared Hank Gardner. 'When yuh make a promise like that, only thing to do is keep it.'

'Only mistake Tom made was in runnin' off and hidin',' said Hank's oldest son, Sam. 'He should 'a' called us together and told us the whole story. He was in the right and should 'a' stood his ground; by runnin' he's admittin' himself in the wrong, which he wasn't.'

'If Tom had shot Jonathan he would have stood his ground,' said Kirk. 'That's one reason why I don't believe he did it.'

'I don't believe he shot him either,' said Will Gardner, Sam's younger brother. 'Leastwise, not without givin' him a chance. Tom wasn't built thataway.' Will was Tom's closest friend, and Kirk nodded his agreement and his thanks.

'Wal,' drawled another homesteader, 'no matter who done it or how, it means war on this range. Yuh say it was the JKL that jumped yuh tonight; yuh can bet the M will throw in with 'em. Reckon we got a fight on our hands.'

'It's been brewin' fer some time,' commented another. 'But we licked 'em before and we can do it ag'in.'

'We licked the M before, but now we got 'em both to fight,' corrected the first speaker. 'Only way we can hope to win ag'in both outfits is to lay our plans and work together. I propose that we call a meetin' here and now and figger out ways and means.'

There, amid the smoke and ashes, a compact was renewed and plans to protect their homes were laid. All felt that if the Flying W fell the other homesteads would quickly follow. Tom's band of night riders, young fellows like Sam and Will Gardner, were assigned to patrol the Flying W boundaries, and signals were arranged whereby the homesteaders could be assembled at any point swiftly and efficiently. When they were parting, young Will Gardner drew Kirk to one side.

'Yuh seen Tom?'

'No. I went over to the Bottom, but Jake Benson was there with a posse and I couldn't learn a thing.'

'Go over again—now. It's late, but Rum Blossom keeps open most of the night. Talk to him alone. He's a tough hombre, but he likes Tom.'

Kirk took his advice. When the homesteaders had left, he merely told his father that he was going to look around a bit, and hit the twisting trail to Bates' Bottom. This time he found Shab Townsend and Joel Cord in the place with Rum Blossom, Benson's party having given up their search. The men greeted Kirk gruffly, and Bates set out a tin cup.

'What'll it be this time Kirk?'

'Same as before, with somethin' for a chaser.'

Bates filled the tin cup from a jug. 'Stretch her out and I'll see what I can do about that chaser.'

Kirk felt his pulse quicken; Bates knew what he wanted. The boss rustler nodded to Shab Townsend, who immediately shuffled out of the place.

'What's become of Tanglefoot Tarberry?' asked Kirk casually. 'Still bummin' grubstakes?'

'Last I seen him he was headin' for the JKL on that Jerry hoss that hangs around the settlement. He'd rigged hisself a saddle outa some odds and ends in the barn and reckoned he'd rustle some JKL cows.'

'Haw, haw!' bellowed Joel Cord, 'I got a picture o' that outfit runnin' cows! They're so slow that the critter they rustled would die o' old age before they got it to the border!'

'Must be on their way, for I ain't seen either of them since. The old coot's jest plain loco; I don't believe he'd know free gold if he seen it.'

'I knowed a tenderfoot onct,' said Cord, 'that lugged a sackful o' yaller stuff outa the hills fer nigh to a hundred miles. Hadda cross a desert and throwed away his rifle and grub and finally his canteen so's he could carry that sack. He was stark, ravin' crazy when they found him, but he got well in time and fust thing he yelled fer was his sack. They give it to him, together with the bad news. What he'd lugged all that distance was iron pyrites—fool's gold. He had a relapse immediate.'

Shab Townsend came shuffling back into the saloon. 'All clear,' he reported to Rum Blossom, who explained to Kirk.

90

'Jest hadda make shore yuh wasn't follered. All right, fellers.'

Townsend and Cord promptly stepped forward and raised an end of the heavy plank which formed the top of Bates' makeshift bar. Bates tipped the hogshead upon which one end had rested, and out of the barrel came Tom!

'Cute, ain' it?' inquired Bates proudly. 'Jake was leanin' right against it most of the time. Yuh fellers oughta been here; it was right funny. Thought I'd bust when he stuck his paw down inter Annabelle's bedroom. I was a-prayin' that she'd baptize him.'

Tom straightened, his anxious gaze going to his brother's face. In the boy's eyes was an appeal for sympathy and understanding. Kirk put his arm across his shoulders and led him to a box. 'Sit down, kid, and tell us all about it.'

Tom told them his story, omitting nothing; and when it was finished Kirk breathed a great sigh of relief. It would be easy to fight back now that he knew beyond all doubt that Tom was innocent.

'And you say the jigger that shot Jonathan did it from behind you?'

'From the trees along the overflow where you followed my tracks. I found a place where two hosses were tied, but I lost the trail in the grass.'

'And the second shot was when they tried

to get you.'

'That's right, Kirk. I reckon they figgered if both of us were killed folks would think we shot each other.'

'It wasn't none of the Bottom boys done it,' said Bates positively. 'We hadn't a thing ag'in old Jonathan. My gosh, no! Why should we? Wasn't he a-feedin' us?'

'It was somebody from the M,' said Kirk. 'That cow that was shot and dragged across our line—the slaughtered steer—it all wears the same brand, and that brand's got to be an M. Only thing that has me guessin' is why they didn't find the head and hide under that brush pile.'

'Kirk, that's what puzzles me, too. I'd swear that Ham Turner expected to find it there. He acted like he couldn't believe his senses when Slim and Tex couldn't find anything.'

Kirk got to his feet. 'There's a heap of things that Ham Turner's goin' to explain to me some day, probably at the point of a gun. But what we got to think about now is how to protect you, Tom. You can't face a murder charge now; the evidence is dead against you and the way folks feel you couldn't get a fair trial. You'll have to stay on the dodge, boy, until we find out who did kill Jonathan Lane.'

'He's safe enough here at the Bottom,' assured Bates. 'He can stay in the storeroom, and if anybody comes snoopin' around the boys'll let me know in plenty of time to stuff him inter thet barrel. He fits it like a foot fits a boot.'

'Thanks, Bates. Tom, you got any money?'

'Couple of dollars; but that's all right. Just tell Dad—'

'You bet I will! But you got to have some money in case you have to get out of this country in a hurry. No tellin' what's goin' to turn up. I'll bring you some the next time I come. So long, feller. Keep yore chin up.'

'I will, Kirk. Godfrey, I wish I had my fingers on the throat of the jasper who shot Jonathan! He'd found out about that steer and had come back to tell me; and then before he could speak—' He broke off abruptly. 'I reckon Nellie thinks I did it, don't she, Kirk?'

'No, I don't believe she does. The way Miss Stacy talked she don't. But in any event it'll straighten out in the end, Tommy. Take it easy now.'

Kirk rode home in a lighter frame of mind. Tom was safe, he felt sure; but the knowledge that the boy was also innocent transcended everything else. Dawn was very close when he reached the cabin, but he awakened his father and told him the news. It acted on Asa Woodward like a strong tonic.

'Then the boy didn't do it! Thank God for that! Kirk, I misjudged him. God forgive me, I did! But he's so hot-headed and quick to flare that I thought shore—Wal, that's off our minds. We must work now to find out who did kill Jonathan.' He sank back in his bunk with a sigh of relief, and Kirk went to the fireplace and removed the stone which covered the opening where he kept his money. He felt for the bag, failed to find it and struck a match. Then he stared at the hole until the match burned his fingers.

'Dad,' he asked, 'did you take my money out of the cache?'

'No, Kirk, I didn't. It's yores, and you know I never bother it.'

Kirk's face was sober as he replaced the stone. Besides his father and Tom there was but one man who had knowledge of the hiding place. That man was Tanglefoot Tarberry.

The funeral of Jonathan Lane was held the next afternoon. It was an imposing affair, attended by all the bigwigs of Mustang County. Judge Kelly was there, fat and pompous and arrayed once more in his swallowtail coat; Jake Benson had left his posse in charge of Skinny Singleton in order to attend; Ham Turner was present with Gault and the whole Monarch crew. All the stores in town were closed out of respect for Lane's memory, and a cowboy had ridden half the night in order to fetch a minister from Chola.

Ham had secured the privilege of riding

with the grief-stricken Barbara. Very quiet and decorous he was, his grave face reflecting just the proper shade of sympathy and consideration as he helped her into and out of the carriage. With them rode Nellie and Vivian, and occasionally the curl on the lips of the Eastern girl became more pronounced as she observed the way in which Ham danced attendance on Barbara. Vivian's experience with men was considerably greater than Barbara's and Turner's veneer was beginning to peel under her searching scrutiny.

As there was no church in Mustang, the services were held at the little cemetery behind the town. The procession which started at the Lane ranch house was augmented as it reached the town, and when the long line of carriages and horsemen passed along the street Kirk Woodward and his father drew their mounts to one side and respectfully removed their hats. Vivian nodded gravely to Kirk, but Barbara turned her head away, biting her lip. To her their action savored of hypocrisy. Ham Turner glared at them, and Jake Benson, riding with Judge Kelly, growled an oath under his breath. The JKL cowboys rode by with faces straight to the front.

When the services were concluded, Ham found an opportunity to speak a word to Judge Kelly. 'I've some business to discuss with you, Judge, as soon as possible. Suppose I stop around to see you after I've taken Barbara home?'

Kelly acquiesced suavely. He had been expecting some sort of overture from this ambitious young manager of The Monarch Cattle Company. When a few hours later he ushered Ham into his living room he was the personification of bluff hospitality.

'Let me have your hat and gloves, Mr. Turner. Sit right down there in that big chair. You'll find cigars beside you—light one and relax. Quite a strain, I take it, acting as escort to our poor little Barbara. Her grief, so nobly restrained, touched me; touched me deeply.'

Ham agreed and lighted a cigar. Kelly disposed of the creamy Stetson hat and buckskin riding gloves and oozed into another capacious chair. He folded his hands before his fat stomach. 'A great loss to the community, a terrible loss. Jonathan Lane was our foremost citizen; we all loved him dearly. I'm afraid things won't be quite the same without him.'

Ham slanted him a probing glance. This was rank hypocrisy and he recognized it as such, having dealt in it himself. He decided that Judge Kelly would be a sympathetic listener to what he had to say.

'You're quite right, Judge. Jonathan Lane was a power in the community. He controlled the destiny of the town, regulated its policies and, I believe, with all deference to you, let his influence be felt even in your court. He was a dictator, but a benevolent one; but now he's gone and there arises the question of his successor. That's why I came to see you. I believe I have the qualifications that you—ah—expect in such a person.'

The judge nodded encouragingly. 'I've had you under observation for some time, my dear Turner. I've marked your ability and—ah—business acumen, and I'm inclined to listen favorably to whatever recommendations you might care to submit. Please speak frankly.'

Their glances met and clung, and perhaps each looked into the warped soul of the other and recognized a kindred spirit. Ham leaned forward in his chair. 'I believe you are the administrator of Lane's estate?'

The judge nodded. 'I was so honored by dear Jonathan.'

'In that case,' said Ham, 'we can talk business.'

Then and there began a conclave which lasted until supper time and was resumed after Ham had partaken of the judge's hospitality. They talked long and earnestly, and as they talked, bit by bit the veneer of honesty and respectability was stripped away and each was exposed to the other as the thief and vulture he was.

At the end of the conference the judge

summed up. 'Your ambition is laudable. Your desire to control a whole county, to build a cow kingdom second to none in the Union shows an ambition that I sincerely admire. As for my part, I am getting no younger and the arduous task of riding circuit and dispensing justice no longer appeals to me. I long for retirement, and if you are successful the—ah—honorarium you mention would go far towards its realization.'

'Go far? Man, with what I'm offering you, you could go East—'

The judge cut in dryly. 'I'd have to go somewhere, and in a hurry, if I agree to do the half of what you want me to!'

'Remember the compensation.'

'Ah, yes, the compensation. Money talks, and I have ever found her voice most pleasing. You may count on me, Hamilton, to the very limit.'

They shook hands solemnly, their eyes glinting with avarice.

Ham remained as the judge's guest overnight, and immediately after breakfast the next morning paid a call on Sheriff Jake Benson. Jake was in his office cleaning up a few odd jobs before riding out with his posse. Ham closed the door behind him and made sure that nobody was within earshot. He declined Benson's invitation to have a chair. Benson, who kept a finger on the pulse of the town, knew of Ham's long visit with the

98

judge.

'I'm not remaining long, Jake. I dropped in to tell you that the judge and I have had an understanding. We find ourselves in complete accord. I am going to try to take the place in the community once held by our late friend, Jonathan Lane. The judge has spoken warmly of you, and I'm sure we're going to get along very well indeed. Our first desire, of course, is to apprehend the murderer of Lane, and we're looking to you to do that little chore. Take the boy alive, if possible; we must make an example of him. If you succeed in your task the judge and I would feel that you are entitled to a substantial reward. In the meanwhile, as evidence of our confidence, I want you to accept this little donation.'

He slipped a folded bank note under Jake's inkwell and turned to the door. Jake got a glimpse of the denomination of the bill and bounced to his feet. With a speed that was startling for a man of his build he beat Ham to the door and opened it for him. With a gentle smile of appreciation, Ham passed outside. That took care of Jake Benson.

He found Stoney Stone and Virgil Depew in a saloon and started at once for the M. He did not stop off at the JKL, but continued on and past the Flying W. When he reached the trail on the far side of the creek he halted and looked towards the distant Flying W headquarters. The cabin still stood but the other buildings were a mass of blackened embers. Two men worked among the debris, and he guessed correctly that they were Kirk Woodward and his father.

He rode on, his mind busy with the future. At the house he was met by Sarge Gault, and after dismissing Stone and Depew, Ham motioned his foreman to follow him into the little office. Sarge straddled a chair.

'Everything all right?'

Ham smiled. 'Right as rain. The judge and I reached an understanding and Jake Benson is in the bag. The first step in our plan is to get the homesteads to the north, and to do that it will be necessary to crush the Woodwards. The JKL is in a fighting mood, and it shouldn't take much of a spark to touch off the powder keg, eh?'

'No, just a little would do it.' They looked across the desk at each other, both thinking hard; and presently Gault leaned forward, his eyes narrowed and glinting. 'Speakin' of sparks, listen!'

Ham listened carefully and nodded his approval. 'You'll have to be careful,' he warned.

'Just fix it so I can get inside for a few minutes and yuh can leave it to me,' he promised.

It was well past midnight when the thunder of approaching hoofbeats awoke Kirk. Thinking it was a guard with the alarm, he called to his father, leaped from the bunk and grabbed his rifle. Half dressed, they rushed out into the yard just as a mounted man pulled up and hailed them.

'Kirk! Godfrey, man, come around here where yuh can see!'

Kirk strode to where young Will Gardner sat his horse, pointing. He looked towards the west. The trees shut off the view, but beyond them the sky was red.

'The JKL!' cried Kirk. 'Will, who would do a trick like that?'

'I don't know, but I do know who's gonna be blamed for it!'

'Signal the rest of the boys. Get them here as quick as you can!'

Will wheeled his horse and spurred out the yard while Kirk ran to the corral. In less than three minutes he was riding towards the creek as rapidly as his pony could carry him. A great anxiety gripped him. Regardless of the fact that he was treading on forbidden ground, he splashed his horse across the stream and sent him lunging up the opposite bank to the JKL range. Once beyond the fringe of cottonwoods he could see plainly.

'Good Lord!' he exclaimed. 'It's the *house!*'

He struck the horse with his spurs and sent him leaping forward. In that house were Barbara and Nellie and—Vivian!

CHAPTER EIGHT

He rode hard, impelled by some force that he did not understand nor attempt to analyze. Burning property in a war like this was all right so long as the lives of men only were endangered, but this house contained the three girls and their Mexican servants. If this was the work of some hot-headed homesteader, Kirk determined that he should answer for it.

The flames mounted higher as he approached and he could see men carrying articles of furnishing and personal belongings from the house. He checked his horse, suddenly aware that he was within the circle of firelight and discernible to any who might chance to look. One did look. As he was backing his horse into the shadows he had a glimpse of Vivian Stacy's face and caught her swift motion for him to retreat.

At a safe distance he halted his horse and dismounted, his eyes searching the milling crowd for a glimpse of the other girls. Then he saw Vivian approaching by a circuitous route and a few minutes later she was at his side.

'Are you completely crazy?' she asked sharply. 'Any one of them will shoot you like a wolf if they happen to see you.'

'Are Nellie and Barbara safe?'

'Of course. The fire started somewhere in the roof and we had ample time to get out. It spread so quickly, though, that nothing could be done. I don't have to ask you if it was you who started it, for I know it wasn't. I don't believe you knew anything about it.'

'I didn't, though why you should believe me I don't know. Yore people burned us out last night.'

'I know. It was shameful. But Barbara's convinced that your brother killed Mr. Lane and is determined to make you pay for it. It's useless to try to argue with her now. She's bitter. Now please go, and don't come back. We're all safe and there isn't a thing you can do.'

'There's just one thing more. I want to talk with Nellie. Will you bring her to that little clump of trees over there?'

She shook her head despairingly. 'Kirk Woodward, if you had a grain of sense you'd get off this place just as quickly as you could. Can't I deliver a message for you?'

'I'd rather talk to her personally. It means quite a lot, Miss Stacy. Please fetch her.'

'I shouldn't, but if I refuse I suppose you'll go looking for her yourself. Wait back there among the trees, and for heaven's sake don't let anybody see you.' She hurried away and Kirk led his horse back into the shadows of the cottonwood grove.

103

He waited patiently for some ten minutes while the flames crackled and roared and the raised voices of the fire-fighters reached him; then he caught sight of two slim figures and went to the edge of the trees to meet them. At sight of him Nellie stopped abruptly, her eyes going wide, and for a moment Kirk thought she was about to turn away.

He spoke quickly. 'Nellie! Don't go. I have somethin' mighty important to tell you. Please listen to me.'

'Kirk, I—'

'It's about Tom. Nellie, he didn't shoot yore father—I know he didn't.' She raised a hand as though to brush the statement aside, and he went on. 'It isn't a guess or hearsay; I know for certain that he didn't do it. Nellie, he needs yore faith so much! Won't you listen?'

She moved slowly towards him. 'You say—you're *sure?*'

'I'm absolutely certain. Come, Miss Stacy, you must hear this, too.'

'Then we'd better move farther back into the trees,' said the Eastern girl. 'I hope you realize what this means to Nellie if Barbara were to know that she's meeting you.'

Kirk spoke a bit sharply. 'I know well enough, but I'm tired of bein' treated like a sneak thief or somethin' else unfit to be seen in human company. I've been patient because I can see the thing through Barbara's eyes, but the Woodwards are innocent of any wrongdoin' of any kind whatever and I'm not goin' to lie down and let folks walk over me. Nellie, there was a time when you believed in me; I'm askin' you to keep on believin' in me and in Tom. The boy idolizes you; he's wild and reckless, but he'd lay down his life in a minute to save you pain. How in the world can you think that he'd grieve you by shootin' yore father?'

For a moment she broke. 'Oh, Kirk, I don't believe he did it! I *don't!* But Barbara keeps reminding me—' She stopped abruptly, regained her control and went on in a dead voice. 'What is it you want to tell me?'

'That's better! Nellie, I always knew you were a soldier. Now listen to me. I saw Tom this mornin'. Never mind how or where; the secret's best kept if nobody but me knows it. He told me the whole story. Nellie, yore father did ride to the Flyin' W and Tom did halt him with a leveled rifle; but Jonathan had his hands in the air and he called to Tom that he'd come to apologize.'

'Apologize!'

'That's dead right. Tom said, "You found out about that slaughtered steer?" and Jonathan said, "Yes, I found—" and just at that moment somebody near the water hole 'way behind Tom shot him. There were two shots, you know. That was the first one; the second one came from the same place just as

Tom wheeled his hoss. If he hadn't turned right sharp, that second shot would have got him. Nellie, that's the truth!'

'Oh, Kirk! Is it—really?'

'Yes. The story rings true. Think! You know what a good rifle shot Tom is; at that distance would he need to fire *twice?* How can you explain that second shot if it wasn't fired at Tom? Well, the boy found yore father dead and cut right over to the water hole, but all he could find was the place where two hosses had been tied. I verified the story by lookin' myself. The tracks were there, and I even found where two men laid in the bushes at the top of the bank. But there wasn't a thing to tell me who they were or where they came from. When Tom started back he heard yore crew. They'd just found Jonathan and he knew they'd never believe his story after the threat all of them had heard him make. So the boy got scared and lit out. And now—well, he's heart-broken. Not so much because of his own danger, but because he figures that you'll lose faith in him.'

'No, Kirk! No! Tell him I believe in him. Something all along told me that he didn't do it. I believe in him, Kirk. Tell him that I do!' In her earnestness Nellie stepped forward and laid a hand on his arm, and even in the darkness he could see the shine of her eyes.

'Bless yore heart, of course I will! And it'll make a new man of him. Now keep this to yourselves. Don't tell Barbara; she'll be sure to think it another Woodward lie and no good can come of lettin' her know. In fact, if I can work without the guilty man knowin' that I'm after him I have a much better chance of gettin' the goods on him ... Now I must go, before they miss you and start huntin' for you. But keep yore chin up and we'll pull out of this mess together.' He turned to Vivian. 'Miss Stacy, I shore won't forget yore sympathy and kindness. Maybe some day I can get square with you.'

The directness of his gaze disconcerted her, and Vivian actually blushed. She laughed shortly. 'I happen to have a keen sense of justice and I don't believe you're getting what the Westerners call a square deal. And please dispense with the "Miss". Call me Vivian.'

'Thanks—Vivian. And now, good night.'

'Good night, Kirk,' she answered, and turned away.

Kirk got back to the Flying W just in time to miss the Monarch crew, who came tearing along the road which led to the JKL. When he arrived at the ranch house it was to find most of the homesteaders gathered there.

'Hell to pay now,' said Hank Gardner grimly. 'They'll come bustin' over here jest as shore as cats have kittens as soon as they can leave the fire. Kirk, how we gonna fight 'em?'

'We don't stand a chance in the dark. Come down to the creek, boys.'

107

He set them to gathering dead brush and had them pile it in stacks about a hundred feet apart on the open range east of the brakes; then he formed them in a long line a hundred yards beyond the piles, where they sat their horses and waited. Kirk rode to the house and got a can of kerosene, and when he returned dawn was not far away.

He patroled the creek bank, listening for the sounds which must precede any attack; and presently he heard them—the thud of approaching hoofbeats. Quickly he rode along the piles of brush, pouring a little kerosene at the edge of each. By the time he had finished, the approaching riders were crossing the creek.

He lighted a pine knot which had been drenched with kerosene, leaned from the saddle and ignited the brush in the first pile. Speeding to the next, he repeated the operation, and so on down the line. Then he joined his men.

'Stop them by shootin' their hosses,' he cautioned each in turn. 'Don't shoot at a man unless you have to.'

The brush piles were roaring when the combined JKL and M crews burst from the brakes. The defenders could see them very distinctly, could even pick out individuals in the bright glare of the fires. The blazing brush seemed to disconcert them and they drew rein uncertainly. Kirk saw Sarge Gault riding about, evidently urging the men to advance; but they argued the matter with him, some of them pointing to the darkness beyond the blazing fire and reminding him of the ready rifles waiting there.

Then into the light rode Barbara. She called a few impassioned words to them, inaudible to the homesteaders above the crackling of the burning brush, then snatched off her hat and raised it, wheeling her horse at the same time. The animal reared as he pivoted and when his forefeet hit the ground she struck him with the spurs. With a toss of his head he lunged into full stride, and her men with a great cry sped after her.

Kirk shouted at the top of his voice: 'The hosses! Get hosses! And for Godfrey's sake *don't shoot her!*'

Past the line of fires charged the combined crews, Barbara leading them. Wheeling, Kirk sent his horse plunging to meet her, while a rumbling volley of rifle fire sounded behind him. At that range and with their targets outlined against the firelight very few bullets missed. Kirk saw half a dozen horses go down, while others, less severely hit, became unmanageable. Men were pitched from their mounts and scrambled to their feet to make their way as best they could to the shadows behind the fires. To continue an advance on foot would have been foolhardy.

Kirk was oblivious to what was going on

about him. He was speeding to meet a slender rider who scorned to turn back, whose magnificent horse—the one her father had ridden—came on in great, unbroken strides. Kirk was shouting, 'Barbara! Go back! Are you crazy?' But she did not hear him, or if she did, refused to obey.

Some of her cowboys who were still mounted charged after her, but again the rifles of the homesteaders barked, cutting their horses from under them. Then Kirk and Barbara, now less than twenty yards apart, leaned back on the reins and slid their mounts to a stop, the legs of the riders almost touching.

Kirk had a glimpse of her, a glimpse that showed him stormy eyes in a set face framed by a halo of dark mist that was her hair, then the flickering firelight flashed on the barrel of her gun as she raised and leveled it. He dived from the saddle, ducking low. He heard the report, felt the hat snatched from his head, saw the flare of the discharge almost in his face. He struck her hard, his arms going about her waist. As the gelding leaped sideways he jerked her from the saddle.

For a moment he held her, but the close embrace was far from a loving one. She had dropped her gun and now beat at him with her fists, kicked him in the shins as hard as she could kick. He set her on her feet and pushed her roughly from him.

'Brute!' she blazed.

'Brute, beast or cad,' he said angrily, 'I have a longin' to wear my hide a bit longer, and you would have shot me. You crazy little fool! What's the idea of chargin' out in the open like you did? If my men hadn't been straight shooters in both senses of the word you would have been killed.'

She stood there straight and defiant, glaring at him. 'Why didn't they try to kill me? I was sure *you* would! Anybody who would burn women in their homes—'

'If I could have been shore of my aim from a runnin' hoss I might have tried it,' he replied fiercely. 'But I was afraid of hittin' the hoss. He was yore father's and Jonathan loved him. Now get in that saddle and make tracks out of here before I forget you're an amateur Eastern society lady and turn you over my knee and paddle you. Go on—scat!'

The look she gave him would have shriveled a cactus, and the only reason she did not speak was that she couldn't think of anything sufficiently scathing to say; but he glared back at her just as fiercely, and finally she turned to the waiting horse and mounted. Her hand fell on the quirt which hung from the horn, and on a sudden impulse she gripped it, spurred close to him and struck him full across the face with the leather thong.

He made no move to dodge; just stood

there looking up at her. Barbara, with a bitter little exclamation, reined the gelding about and rode rapidly towards the creek. Even then she heard Kirk's clear voice as he ordered his men to hold their fire. Her cheeks were wet with angry tears. If only they would shoot at her!

She was met by Ham Turner, who had kept well in the background. 'Are you hurt?' he asked solicitously, and for the first time Barbara was guilty of giving him a curt answer.

Gault came limping up to address Turner. 'Told yuh they'd be layin' for us. We played right into their hands. Half of our hosses are dead or hurt too bad to ride. We better pull outa here.'

'It's that damned Kirk Woodward,' said Ham bitterly. 'Nobody but he would have thought to build those fires.' He led the way back to the JKL in company with the still angry Barbara. Ham had not joined in the charge and he had the uneasy feeling that he had suffered in Barbara's eyes because of that. He attempted to make up for it by showing even more than his usual consideration.

'Now that the cowards have burned you out, you must come over to the M. My house is entirely yours, of course.'

'Thanks, I'll remain on the JKL,' she said shortly. 'We'll rebuild at once. In the meantime we can use the foreman's cabin.'

'It was a dastardly act, Barbara. I'll make the Woodwards pay before I get through with them.'

'I'll take care of the Woodwards. It's our fight—Dad's fight. If he were living he'd never quit until they were licked. I'm his daughter.'

She was very much in earnest. Her face was bleak at thought of her father's death at the hands of Tom Woodward; her blood boiled at this last outrage, committed almost before he was cold in his grave. The fact that the Woodwards might have had no hand in the firing of the house meant nothing to her; they were nesters and if they themselves were innocent one of their clique was certainly guilty. The fire had been deliberately set, for now she recalled that just before the fire she had smelled the odor of kerosene. Since the nesters were guilty they must pay, and since the Woodwards were the backbone of their defense the Woodwards must go first.

By riding double, the men of both crews got back to the JKL. Here they remained the rest of the night, for fresh horses could not be caught up until the next day. The girls established themselves in Slim Chance's cabin, and Ham selected a small room in the barn for his headquarters. A burning rage possessed him, for it was he who had suggested the raid to Barbara and the stinging

113

defeat at the hands of Kirk Woodward rankled. He sent at once for Virg Depew, Stoney Stone, and Sarge Gault, and when they presented themselves he lost no time in making plain to them what he expected them to do.

'It's clear that the Woodwards set that fire tonight,' he told them. 'Nobody else would have had any motive. But as usual they left no proof and therefore are out of reach of the law. But they're not going to get away with it. Kirk Woodward must go.'

The lazy appearing Depew yawned. 'If yuh had said the word the other night—'

'Things have happened since that weren't on the books then. Also there were women in the room. I'm giving you that word now. I want you boys to take some men to Mustang. Gault, you're in charge. Wait there until Kirk Woodward shows up if it takes a month. Then see to it that he doesn't leave town—unless it's feet first.'

'When do we start?' asked Stone.

'Right now. Stay at the hotel at my expense and frame it any way you like. Don't make it too raw, but in any event you'll be protected. The main thing is to get Kirk Woodward, and I'll pay the man that fixes his clock one hundred dollars.'

He dismissed them, but Gault lingered for a moment.

'What do you think of it?' asked Ham.

114

Sarge shrugged. 'Woodward's gotta go, all right; but it mighta been safer and surer if you laid out in the brush somewhere and potted him as he rode by.'

'Too raw. It would make a hero of him.'

'Also a corpse—which is the main thing. I tell yuh, that feller's got all the luck with him. Look at the dead cow and the butchered steer; he beat us both times.'

'You're overly pessimistic, Sarge. What good is his luck going to do him against gunmen like Depew and Stone, to say nothing of yourself and the boys you take with you?'

'Wal-l-l, not much, I reckon, even if he is a pretty good hand with a short gun himself. But when I want to get rid of a feller I do it without the fancy trimmin's. Lay for him and let him have it—that's my way.'

Their glances met and held, and the chances are that both were thinking of Jonathan Lane.

CHAPTER NINE

Kirk and the homesteaders remained on guard until daylight. By that time there was no sign of the enemy save the dead horses they had left behind them. These were buried, after which Kirk assembled his little band and addressed them sternly. 'Now I'm ready to lick the one who started the JKL fire, if he's man enough to own up to it.'

They looked at each other blankly.

'Do yuh mean to tell us that yuh didn't start it yoreself?' blurted Hank Gardner.

'If I didn't know you said that without thinkin', I'd start in by tacklin' you,' Kirk told him sharply. 'I'm not so lowdown that I'd burn women out of their home.'

'Mebbe I did spill over at the mouth too quick,' admitted Hank. 'As to the fire, it wasn't me or my boys. I can swear to that.'

The others were equally insistent that they had no hand in the thing, and Kirk was finally forced to drop the matter. It was possible that the fire was due to natural causes, but unless they were plainly apparent the JKL must believe it was set in retaliation for the firing of the Flying W buildings.

When his neighbors had departed for their homes, Kirk spoke to his father. 'The law is a joke in Mustang and we can expect no protection from Jake Benson; but just the same we must report the attack to him and give him the chance to refuse to help us. He's probably out searchin' for Tom now, but he ought to be in town tonight. I'll ride in after supper and see him.'

'We'd better both go. From here on neither of us must travel alone. Kirk, who could have set that fire?'

'If Jonathan Lane had lived one minute longer he would have told Tom who butchered that steer. Then we'd have a pretty good idea who set the fire. We didn't set it, nor any of our homesteader friends. If it was set at all, there's only one answer left.'

'The M?'

'That's my hunch.'

'Still aimin' to stir up trouble, huh? Lane's boys never did come right out and fight us, and the M know they cain't lick us alone.'

'If my hunch is right, Ham Turner is usin' the JKL to fight his own battles. The killin' of Jonathan wasn't enough. Slim Chance and the JKL crew have laid that against Tom, and Slim told us that he didn't believe you or I had anything to do with it. But this firin' of the house can be blamed direct on us homesteaders and the fact that Barbara and Nellie and Miss Stacy might have burned in their beds was enough to send the JKL boys against us ... Well, I'll run over to the Bottom and see Tom. You better let me have some money for him in case he has to pull out suddenlike. I had some under that stone on the hearth, but it's gone.'

'Then it musta been taken by the JKL men when they were snoopin' around lookin' for that hide.'

Kirk was still inclined to lay the blame on old Tanglefoot Tarberry, but said nothing about it to his father. He rode over to the

117

Bottom and Bates admitted him to the storeroom where Tom was hiding. 'We only pack him in the bar'l when somebody we don't know shows up,' Rum Blossom explained.

Kirk talked with the boy for half an hour, giving him the latest news and trying to cheer him up. 'It'll work out all right, kid. One of these days somebody's goin' to take a misstep and then we'll nail him dead to rights. Now here's somethin' I saved for the last: I talked to Nellie last night and she asked me to tell you that she believed in you. Tom, she's a girl in a billion!'

'She did? She told you that? Gosh, Kirk! Thanks! Knowin' that Nellie's with me is mighty comfortin', but it galls me to have to hide out like I was guilty while you and Pa have this fight on yore hands. All on account of me.'

'Nothin' of the sort. If that killin' was framed—which we figure it was—the victim might have been Dad or me as easily as it was you. Just you take it easy, and if things get too tight Bates will see that you get away and you have enough money to last you for a while.'

He rode home in moody silence, worried and perplexed. The satisfaction gained from the knowledge of Tom's innocence was overshadowed by thought of the boy's danger. The men who frequented the Bottom

118

were thieves and worse; it was quite conceivable that one of them would be tempted to betray Tom's hiding place, and once in the hands of Jake Benson and Judge Kelly there was no doubt of the outcome.

At dusk that evening Kirk and his father started for Mustang, explaining to the homesteaders who were riding line and cautioning them against a surprise. They used the upper road, a trail which ran directly to Mustang from the claim of Hank Gardner to the north of them. The country they crossed was all open range without cover for bushwhackers and they met no one until they entered the town.

Once in Mustang Kirk was gripped with a premonition of brewing trouble. It was just an intangible hunch and he did not even mention it to his father; but he redoubled his caution and scanned every opening they passed.

It was now quite dark and the people on the street could be recognized only when they passed a lighted window or beneath the kerosene flares over the doorways of shop and store. Out in the middle of the street where Kirk and his father rode, recognition would be impossible; nevertheless, that feeling of uneasiness persisted. They reached the sheriff's office and pulled over to the hitching rack, dismounted and tied. A pale light showed through the window of the place.

Kirk pushed open the door and they entered. The office was empty. Jake Benson, seeing them at the hitching rack and guessing what had brought them, had hastily left by the back door. In the alley he found a Monarch cowboy, one of those brought to town by Sarge Gault.

'Woodward just come in,' Benson told him briefly, and continued on his way. His part of the job was to be somewhere else if anything happened. The cowboy hurried down the alley to a saloon, entered by the back door and reported to his companions. In all there were eight of them, and they immediately left by the way he had entered.

In the alley they talked it over briefly. All their plans had been made, but there must be no slip. In a body they made their way along the alley to the general store owned by Jonathan Lane, where they separated. Two of the M cowboys remained in its rear; two more took stations in the passageways which separated the store from the buildings on either side; Depew, Stone, Gault, and the remaining cowboy went to the front of the building.

Gault stationed himself at a corner, Stone walked to a horse which was tied at the hitching rack, the cowboy went down the street towards the sheriff's office. Virgil Depew entered the store. There was nobody inside but the storekeeper and to him Depew said, 'Git!' The man gave him an apprehensive glance and left the place. Depew went into a corner, hitched his guns into the proper place for a quick draw, and leaned against the wall. The place was completely covered, inside and out.

Back in the sheriff's office, Kirk and his father awaited Benson's return. Kirk was still apprehensive and uneasy, and this seemed about as safe a place to be as they could select. The absence of the sheriff was not unusual; he might have recently returned to town and gone to the hotel for a belated supper.

After some ten minutes or so the door opened and a man shoved his head through the opening and looked about. Kirk recognized him as a Monarch rider.

'Jake not back yet?' he asked.

Kirk answered. 'No. Have you any idea where he is?'

'Shore. Seen him up at the store a few minutes ago. I'll be back later.' He closed the door and went up the street.

They waited a while longer, then Kirk said to his father, 'You stay here in case I miss him. I'll stroll up to the store and see if I can round him up.'

'Buy a couple boxes of cartridges while yuh're there.'

Kirk left the office and walked slowly along the sidewalk, treading the planks like a wary

121

cougar and dodging the occasional patches of light. He reached the store, a large frame building with an upper story and a small cellar. At the hitching rack outside he could see a man either tying or untying a horse, but he was outside the light and Kirk could not identify him. He started up the six long steps to the store entrance.

'What's that yuh called me?'

Kirk turned. The man who had been at the hitching rack was now at the bottom of the steps. His face was twisted angrily and he glared up at Kirk. Woodward recognized him now.

'Haven't said a word, Stoney. You're hearin' things.'

He entered the store, and the moment he did so he knew he had walked into a trap.

There was nobody in sight, not even the storekeeper; but as he walked slowly to the middle of the room he felt a presence behind him and turned slowly as though looking for somebody to wait on him. Facing him, a little to one side of the doorway, was Virgil Depew. He was standing clear, arms hanging at his sides, their elbows slightly bent.

'I wanta know what yuh called me out there!'

It was Stone. He had stepped to the doorway, a vague form against the outside blackness. Depew, also in the shadow, tensed slightly. Kirk stood directly under one of the hanging kerosene lamps.

Although Woodward knew that the hand of death was about to snatch at him, he remained cool. He even found time to fathom their plan. The loud-mouthed, comparatively clumsy Stone would force a fight, and when Kirk made his move Virg Depew would shoot him. A quick exchange of guns and Stone would be prepared to say that he had shot Kirk. Depew would be the witness to the 'insult' as well as to the fact that Kirk had drawn first. Not too raw that way.

Cringing would never do, nor would delay. Kirk spoke coldly.

'Reckon you misunderstood me, Stone. I wasn't talkin' just to you. I said *the two of you were a pair of white-livered skunks!*'

He spoke to Stone, but his gaze was on Depew, and he did not give the gunman the slightest advantage. Depew was just about the fastest man with a gun in that neck of the woods. Kirk jerked his Colt and fired from the hip, and he did it just in time, for Depew's guns were out of their holsters and snapping upward as he released the hammer. And almost in the same instant Kirk literally dove for an opening between the counters.

Depew's guns exploded, but they did not have sufficient elevation, and the slugs drilled into the floor where Kirk's feet had been. Stone, not having planned to draw at all, stood frozen for the half-second necessary for

Kirk to get in motion. He himself was no slouch with a six-gun and when he did drag his hardware it was with the ease and swiftness of long practice; but Kirk was in mid-air as he fired and his bullet merely knocked off a boot heel as Woodward disappeared behind the counter.

In the next second Virgil Depew hit the floor, dead.

Stone leaped backward from the doorway, nearly falling down the steps in his haste. The tables had been completely turned and it was now Kirk who held the advantage. 'Woodward shot Virg!' yelled Stone. 'Watch that back door, yuh fellers!'

Sarge Gault came up at a run, his military mind grasping the situation instantly. 'He cain't get out,' he said. 'We got him trapped. Come on!'

He leaped up the steps and stopped at the doorway, but a quick glance about the lighted interior failed to reveal any sign of Kirk. Dropping to hands and knees, Gault crawled into the room, heading for the near end of the counter behind which Kirk had disappeared. At his quick order, Stone moved in like fashion to the counter on the opposite side of the room. Extending his gun into the aisle behind the counter, Gault fired two shots. Cautiously he peered around the end. The aisle was clear to the end of the room. He stood up and watched as Stone repeated the operation on his side.

'Everything clear,' reported Stone.

Gault glanced about him. The counters ended at a partition which extended across the rear of the room. Kirk was not behind the counters and there was no hiding place in the space between them.

'Must be behind that partition,' said Gault. 'Go up the aisle back of the counter. Watch the openin' between the counters on my side and I'll do the same for you.' It was the soldier, the strategist, giving the orders.

They advanced slowly, keen eyes restless and roving, guns extended before them. They reached the break in the middle of the counters without seeing their quarry. There was no doubt whatever that Kirk had passed behind the partition.

They went as close to this as they dared, exchanging understanding glances, and at Gault's swift nod leaped around the partition and into the space behind it. Crouched and tense they stood, guns leveled. Kirk Woodward was not there!

Gault slowly straightened and looked about him. Woodward had not left by the front door and two men guarded the back. The windows were tight in their frames, and a man guarded each side. He must still be in the store. A flight of steps led to the upper story and the door at their head was closed. In the floor was a hinged trapdoor which opened on the steps leading to the cellar.

Stone, having followed the direction of his glances, spoke apprehensively. 'Gonna be kinda tough tacklin' him if he's upstairs or down in that cellar, ain't it?'

Gault stood thinking for a moment. 'Find a hammer and some twentypenny-nails.' He stood watching until Stone returned. 'Spike that trapdoor down,' was the curt order. When Stone had obeyed, Gault sent him to the head of the stairs to nail the door shut.

'That'll hold him. Now go outside and tell the boys to watch close—doors, windows, every openin'. Even the roof. These alleys are wide and there's a drop of a story on each side, but the danged fool might try to jump.'

Stone went out. Gault worked swiftly now. His poker face was as imperturbable as ever but his eyes were glinting with a sinister purpose. In front of the partition was a drum of kerosene; with one mighty heave he overturned it and the oil flowed over the floor in a quickly spreading stream. He ran ahead of it, stopped near the doorway and turned. His gun flashed upward and roared; and the lamp chimney shattered to bits, the wick flame leaping high. Again he fired, smashing the burner and puncturing the bowl. The lamp swung crazily, oil spurting from it. There was a flare as the liquid caught and a burning drop splashed into the pool beneath.

Gault leaped from the room, bounding

down the steps. Behind him there sounded a great *woosh!* and a cloud of black smoke belched from the doorway. In a breath the whole interior was a mass of flame, roaring, swirling from one end of the building to the other.

'What in hell yuh done?' gasped Stone.

Gault had no intention of taking this man into his confidence. 'It wasn't me. The danged fool was hidin' behind the oil bar'l. Knocked it over and spilled the oil all over the floor. Then he tried to shoot out the light. Go round to the back and tell the boys to keep their eyes peeled.'

Within the space of a few seconds the place was a furnace. Instantly the town awoke, men coming from every direction. The rim of a locomotive wheel, suspended before the blacksmith shop, pealed forth its rallying call under the strokes of a sledge. Bucket brigades were formed, pumps manned.

Fed by the burning oil, the flames raged, and they might as well have used tin cups in their effort to extinguish them. In a very short time it became apparent that the store was doomed, and men began wetting down adjoining buildings; but the passageways which separated them from the burning building proved no obstacle to the spread of the fire and soon the entire block of sunblasted structures on that side of the street were ablaze.

127

In this beehive of action there were some drones. They came from the M and they stood as close to the flames as the heat would permit, watching, waiting, hands on their guns. If Kirk escaped the flames he must surely perish under the flailing lead from their weapons.

Through the night the conflagration raged. The JKL crew arrived with Barbara leading them; practically all the homesteaders except a few left on guard came in; Ham Turner came racing with the rest of the M outfit. A few men doggedly tossed buckets of water, but most of them were busy salvaging what they could from the flames, praying in the meanwhile that the fire would burn itself out without completely destroying the town. Not until after dawn were they assured that the destruction would be confined to the one block.

Asa Woodward sat on the edge of a watering trough across the street from the gutted store, his face grey and haggard, his hair singed, his clothes blackened and burned. Three times he had tried to pierce the flames in an effort to find his son, and three times he had collapsed and had been dragged to safety. Now he sat in a huddle, stunned and apathetic. One son outlawed, the other without any doubt burned to a crisp in that raging hell.

Barbara Lane stood some distance away

from Asa with Ham Turner, Judge Kelly, and Sheriff Benson. Word that Kirk Woodward had been trapped in the store had reached her—Ham had seen to that—and now she stood appalled. Within her was a dull ache that she could not understand and did not try to analyze. She just couldn't make herself believe that he was gone; he had always seemed so alive, so strong, so sure of himself.

'You're sure there's no hope for—him?' she asked Ham in a dead voice.

'Not a chance,' answered Ham gravely. 'He must have been trapped in the midst of that burning oil. Gault said it went up like gunpowder. If only he had used his head instead of trying to shoot out the light!'

She shuddered. 'His poor father!'

'It must have been a horrible death. And the material damage! Store, saddle, shop, feed store—all JKL property. What shall you do?'

'Rebuild, of course. The town needs them all. But to think of Kirk dying like that! It's terrible.'

There was a little sob in her voice and her face was bleak.

Ham glanced at her sharply. 'He was your enemy, and last night you would have shot him. His brother killed your father, Kirk or one of his crowd burned the house over your head. I'd call it just retribution.'

129

She struggled with her emotion, succeeded in conquering it. 'Yes, he was our enemy; but I know he would have wanted to go out fighting, with a smoking gun in his hand.'

As they rode home in the dawn, Ham left her to talk with Gault.

'You sure he didn't get out?'

'How could he? We were watchin' every rathole. I tell yuh, an ant couldn't 'a' crawled outa there without our spottin' it. No sir, yuh can sleep peaceful. Kirk Woodward never got out of that buildin', and there's nothin' left of it or him but some hot ashes.'

Ham breathed a sigh of relief. 'How much of that fire was an accident?'

Gault grinned crookedly. 'Not a danged bit of it! I laid it on Kirk Woodward, o' course; but it was me upset that drum of kerosene and shot out the light—not him. He was hidin' either in the cellar or upstairs, and I had Stoney nail the trapdoor and the door at the head of the steps.'

'Seems to me that with all the men you had you could have rounded him up and blasted him down without taking the chance of destroying the whole town.'

'Shore, we could, but yuh're out to wreck the JKL; ain't yuh? Well, get out yore pencil and paper and figger for yoreself how much cold cash it'll take to rebuild all them stores.'

Turner's eyes glinted and he favored Sarge with an approving smile.

130

'You're a man after my own heart, Gault! We should go far together.'

CHAPTER TEN

When Kirk dived through the opening between the two counters he brought up heavily against a row of shelves. His right foot was numb from the shock of Stone's bullet, but he could not pause to determine the extent of the damage. Getting to his knees, he turned so as to face the front of the store and started moving backwards along the aisle.

He heard Stone bolt from the store, heard him shout that Depew had been killed. Immediately thereafter came the frantic order to watch the rear door and Kirk knew there was no hope of escape in that direction. He reached the space behind the partition, got up, and found his injuries confined to a missing boot heel.

There were men in the front and men in the back, probably men on both sides of the building. Now that he had killed Depew they had the excuse they needed to shoot him down on sight. If only he could find a place to hold them at bay he might eventually escape with his life; for, prejudiced against homesteaders as they were, the citizens of Mustang would not stand for outright murder.

There was the upstairs; he might hold the door against them for some time. There was also the cellar, and of the two Kirk chose the latter. For one thing he knew there was an outside door which might offer the chance of escape. Crossing the floor he opened the trapdoor. A flight of steep steps led downward, and a candle in its holder stood on the top one. He descended, drawing the trapdoor shut after him.

There were no windows and the gloom was impenetrable. Feeling his way to the slanting outside door, he pushed against it. It was locked, probably by a padlock on the outside.

He went back to the foot of the cellar steps and, gun in hand, stood there looking up at the trapdoor. He heard two men enter the store, heard the shots intended to blast him from behind the counter, heard them pounce into the space over his head. The sound of their voices reached him but not the words. Then came the hammering that told him he was being nailed in the cellar.

This mystified him. Surely they were not planning merely to imprison him. Perhaps they intended to rush him from the outside cellar entrance. If so, it would be suicide for some of them, for he could crouch in a corner and pick them off until his gun was empty.

He was not long left in doubt as to their intentions. Something shook the floor above him, then came the sound of two shots. There was a moment of silence followed by a muffled explosion which rocked the building. And then he heard the snapping and crackling of flames and knew the reason for the nails in the trapdoor. The store had been fired and he was to be destroyed with it.

He ran up the steps and pushed against the trapdoor with all his strength. He might as well have tried to dislodge the great wall of China. Feeling about he found the candle and lighted it. His fingers were shaking. A man can face death at gun or rope with some degree of calmness, but the thought of slowly roasting is enough to unnerve the bravest.

Descending the stairs, he held the light above him and looked around. The cellar was as wide as the building but only ten feet long, having been dug originally for the purpose of storing odds and ends of merchandise and a supply of wood for the winter. There was a break in the stone wall where six steps led to the outside door, but even if he could force this he knew that he would be met with a hail of lead loosed by the men who were watching there.

And then he saw another door!

He ran to it and pulled it open. It was a double door, with an air space between the front and the back, and it opened into a vegetable cellar. Here the produce traded by homesteaders was kept against summer heat and winter cold. The floor was some three feet lower than that on which he stood and the walls and ceiling were shored with heavy timbers. He descended the four steps and pulled the door shut. The crackling in the store above him had become a steady roar and already the cellar he had just quit was becoming warm.

A moment's reflection told him that the door would be no protection when the floor collapsed. He went outside again and after a little search among the stuff with which the cellar was littered found a shovel. With this he reentered the place.

There was but one chance left to him. He started digging away the earth at the back of the cubbyhole and banking the dirt against the door. He worked furiously, presently discarding his coat and shirt. The pile grew, started climbing. The earth was hard and there was the danger of the crust over his head caving in and burying him, but he dared not stop. At last the door was completely covered to a depth of several feet and he sank weakly to the ground and relaxed. When he had regained his breath and some measure of his strength he put on his shirt and coat. He felt reasonably secure.

In his tomb he could not hear the roar of the flames or the shouts of the men who fought them, but from time to time the earth shook about him and he knew that part of the building had collapsed. How long he had been digging he could not even guess. After a while the dirt banked against the door began to steam and the air became warmer. He forced his tired muscles into action and shoveled some more.

And now his mind turned from the necessity of seeking safety to the cause of his predicament. This was murder, deliberately planned and ruthlessly carried out. He had been marked as a target for Virg Depew's guns; that failing, he had been delivered to the flames. Hot anger gripped him at thought of such a diabolical means of removing him.

Who had set the fire he did not know. He had seen but three men—Depew, Stone, and the M cowboy who had indirectly sent him into the trap. He could not believe that Stone had planned this. Stone was too slow-witted to do anything but hunt him down and try to shoot him. Virg Depew never acted on his own responsibility. But the presence of the two in the plot against him suggested Ham Turner. Ham Turner and Sarge Gault. But of course Ham never did anything himself if there was danger connected with it.

The candle sputtered and went out and he knew that a number of hours had passed since he had lighted it; but he also knew that he must remain here until the heat had abated and the Monarch men outside were withdrawn. Presently he slept. He awoke

135

hungry, and feeling about, found some carrots. He pared them with his knife and ate them raw. Surely he was safe enough by this time. He found the shovel and started digging at an upward slant...

★   ★   ★

The JKL and M crews returned to their respective headquarters and, tired out from their exertions, were excused from work for the day. For several hours thereafter a deep silence hung over both spreads.

The three girls on the JKL did not sleep. Nellie, in her room, sat at a window and stared dumbly towards Mustang. A haze of smoke hung over the town, and beneath that pall lay Kirk Woodward, a blackened, shapeless mass that had been a man. So thought Nellie, and with the thought came sobs, the more bitter because of their repression.

In the other bedroom Barbara and Vivian Stacy lay on their bed in the darkened corner, both trying to forget in sleep, both staring wide-eyed at the ceiling above them. The fair Eastern girl had not accompanied the crew to the fire and had learned only a few minutes before of the awful death of Kirk Woodward. It had left her numb.

She was thinking now how strange it was that she had been attracted by this man. At

136

first sight of him her reaction had been one of scorn for his worn clothing, for the very incongruity of his appearance among those who had decked themselves out in their finest. The scorn had soon disappeared. He wore the clothing to which he was accustomed with a greater grace than those who felt the pinch of collar and shoe, the stiffness of starched shirt and store clothes. And he had proven before the night was over that he was all man, the kind of man that women admire, self-assured without being forward, competent, quick-thinking, aggressive, strong.

Each little trick that he had cleverly turned back on his enemies stimulated her amusement and strengthened her admiration. As Barbara had so bitterly told him, he was very sure of himself. And with it all there was no affectation; at all times he was his own simple self. But now he was dead, and the very manner of his death left Vivian wondering if, after all, that holocaust were the result of an accident of his making. Surely he would have dashed through the burning oil and shot his way into the clear rather than supinely submit to such a fate.

Now that she thought of it, she began to wonder at the presence of Gault and Stone and Depew in town when Ham Turner, as he had taken care to inform them, was on the Monarch range. At least one of the three was in constant attendance on Ham; no fighter himself, he must have the protection of hired guns when he ventured abroad. She was too much a stranger in the country even to guess what Ham's motive for removing Kirk Woodward might be, but Ham didn't. So the motive was not jealousy. Greed might be the answer. She had heard Kirk denounce Turner for his ruthlessness in acquiring other homesteads, and had gathered that Ham had tried his best to get the Woodward place. Well, whatever the motive, Vivian decided with a woman's disregard for logic that Ham Turner had been at the bottom of this terrible affair.

She detested Turner. She might not understand the West, but she had a fair understanding of men, and there wasn't a thing about Ham Turner that rang true to her. The supposedly original bits of wit which he sprang on Barbara were recognized by Vivian as having been said by men of his class so many times as to have become not only trite, but tiresome. His little acts of thoughtfulness and consideration she knew to be samples of the stock in trade used by man in his pursuit of woman since the time of Adam. For despite Barbara's Eastern education she was still essentially Western: ingenuous, trusting, frank, utterly unused to deception. But Vivian could not warn her against the man without risking offense.

Barbara, lying beside her, was miserable and depressed without knowing why. She told herself that she hated Kirk Woodward, and that she should feel no regret at his passing; but the days he had reminded her of, the days when they had played together and ridden together and teased and tormented each other, persisted in recurring to her, and now that the companion of those younger and happier days was lying somewhere in the ruins of the gutted store she grieved for him. She bit her lip and blinked at the ceiling, and called on her dead father to make her strong. It was the manner of his passing that affected her so strongly, she told herself. It could be nothing more.

Unable to endure it any longer, she got quietly out of bed and dressed. Once in the kitchen, the rumble of wheels and the voices of men drew her outside. A freighting wagon loaded with building materials had just drawn up before the ruins of the ranch house, and carpenters and masons were preparing to start work on a new structure even before the wreckage of the old one had been completely cleared away. She hurried to join them, thankful for any kind of diversion.

Shortly before noon Ham Turner arrived with his bodyguard, now reduced to the number of one, that one being Stoney Stone. He greeted her cheerfully and for some minutes they discussed plans for the new home. When they finally entered Slim's cabin they found the other two girls up. Nellie, who was preparing dinner, nodded listlessly to him, her lids heavy and red. Vivian deliberately turned her back and strolled to a window, ignoring his greeting completely. Ham frowned; he was beginning to believe that this blonde lady from the East disliked him.

He started a light discourse, patently designed to divert minds from the tragedy of the night before. Barbara did her best to help; the other girls were apathetic. Stone sat in a corner, stiff and stolid. They all heard the measured tread of a horse outside the cabin.

'Probably the judge riding over to see you about the new house,' said Ham. Then a knock sounded, and Barbara opened the door.

'Howdy, folks,' said Kirk Woodward, and stepped inside.

Not a sound greeted him, not even a gasp, so petrified with surprise were they. He acted before they could recover; his gun slipped into his hand and was leveled at Stoney Stone.

'Don't even bat an eye, Stoney, or I'll blow you clear through that wall. Ham, keep yore hands in plain sight. Sit down, ladies. I'm downright sorry to have to do this in yore house but there's no other way I can get yore ear.'

140

'Woodward!' cried Ham. 'Why, bless you, man, we're delighted to see you alive! We thought—'

'Shut up. You're just about as glad as Cain would have been if Abel had got up and offered to shake hands! Please sit down, Barbara; I got some things to say.'

She had been staring at him with parted lips and hands pressed tightly against her bosom. Still staring, she backed slowly to a chair and sat down. Vivian had turned from the window, her face glowing. Nellie, with a glad little cry, came running to him.

'Kirk! It's you! Really you!'

He smiled at her. 'Yes, Nellie. And right off the bat I'm goin' to ask you to do somethin' for me. Run out to the bunkhouse and fetch Slim Chance and the boys.' She lingered for a moment longer, watching him with warm, unbelieving eyes; then, with a little nod, ran from the room. Kirk moved to a corner and pushed a chair into position with his foot, then sat down, the gun resting on his knee.

The heavy tread of booted feet sounded outside and a moment later the JKL boys, led by Chance, came into the room to halt and stare suspiciously.

Kirk spoke calmly, addressing himself to Chance. 'Slim, I came here deliberate, against yore orders, because I had somethin' to say that you boys ought to hear and because I know you're square-shooters enough to listen. If when I get through you want to shoot me, or hang me, or burn me at the stake, you can hop right to it.'

'Start talkin',' said Chance shortly.

'Keno. There's a lot I could say but won't because I have no first-hand knowledge of it and no proof. But there is one thing I can talk about because I happened to be present at the time. That's about last night's fire. Boys, the burnin' of the store was no accident.'

'When a feller upsets a fifty-gallon drum of kerosene and then trys to shoot out a light right over it, I wouldn't call it an accident either.'

'I see you know somethin' about it. Now I'll tell you the truth. That fire was started by somebody from the M after the trapdoor to the cellar where I was hidin' had been nailed shut. In other words, it was started to burn me alive.'

'Why—why!' spluttered Ham Turner.

'Surprised all to death, ain't you, Ham? Well, maybe you are at that; maybe the fire wasn't in the cards to begin with. But I'll do the talkin' for a spell. You just pin yore ears back and listen. Boys, my father and I went to Mustang to report yore attack on the Flyin' W. We didn't expect any help from Jake Benson, but we shore had no idea what we were walkin' into. Benson's office was empty and we settled down to wait for him, and pretty soon an M cowboy poked his head in the door and told us Jake was up at the store. It was the bait, and like a fool I swallowed it. I went up there.

'The minute I walked into the store I smelled a rat. It was Virg Depew. He was standin' to one side of the door and I didn't see him until I was in the middle of the room. Right away Stone stepped into the entrance actin' all cut up about somethin' and demandin' what it was I called him just before I came in. I hadn't said a word.

'The game, you see, was to force me to draw on Stone, after which Virg would plug me. I beat them to it, and instead of watchin' Stone I was watchin' Virg. I got him just in time and dived behind the counter. Stone's bullet tore a heel off my boot.' He raised one foot to show them.

'I heard Stone yell to watch the back and knew I couldn't get out that way. I ducked into the cellar, pullin' the trapdoor shut after me. I heard two men come in and one of them nailed the door down. The outside cellar door was padlocked and even if I had broken out they had men there to shoot me. Then I heard what must have been the drum of coal oil when it was upset and the two shots that fired it, although at the time I didn't know what was goin' on.'

'That ain't so!' blazed the slow-witted Stone. 'Sarge told me you upset that—' He broke off abruptly suddenly aware of what he had said.

'So it was Sarge Gault, huh?' cried Kirk triumphantly. 'That's what I wanted to know. Boys, there she is. Sarge fired that buildin' and left me in it to die. But I found a shovel and a vegetable cellar, and I dug myself in so deep that the fire couldn't reach me. And then I dug myself right out again and rode here hopin' I'd find Stone and Turner so's I could ask them some questions. I reckon I don't need to now. Slim, what is it? Do I go free or do I hang?'

Chance's face was a picture of shocked wrath. 'Stone, yuh dirty rat! If it wasn't for cheatin' Kirk, I'd blast yuh myself! Of course yuh go free, Kirk. By jacks, I never heard anything so low!' His attitude was reflected on the faces of the other JKL cowboys. Kirk got to his feet.

'Thanks, boys. A fair fight is one thing, murder another. And one of the things I know but can't prove is that Tom never shot Jonathan Lane. Ham, you can pass a warnin' along to Gault. Tell him that I aim to shoot him on sight. Ladies, my apologies. Good day.' He backed from the room, closed the door behind him.

There was a moment of silence, then Stone leaped to his feet and moved swiftly to a front window. His gun was in his hand and before Slim's sharp cry of protest could reach him the weapon roared and the pane dissolved in splinters as the bullet crashed through it. And so close to that report that it seemed but an echo came another.

Stone, face twisted in a grimace of hate, rocked back on his heels as though he had been smitten by an invisible maul. The expression of rage faded and for a moment there appeared one of astonishment and unbelief; then the rigid muscles went lax and he slipped down along the wall and lay still.

From without came the measured roll of hoofs, and then silence.

CHAPTER ELEVEN

During the few seconds it took Stone to act out the last scene in his speckled career, not a person in the room moved. At the sound of the shot Ham Turner's muscles tensed as though he were about to leap to safety, the girls stared in horrified fascination, and Slim Chance and his men stood frozen in the inner doorway. It was Slim who broke the silence.

'Well, the lowdown polecat got his!'

As though reminded of Kirk's accusation that the fire had been planned by the M, all eyes went to Turner; and he, knowing they were watching him, gathered his wits for the supreme test. He returned their glances, finally letting his reproachful gaze rest on Barbara.

'I can see that you believe what Woodward said,' he observed quietly. 'I can't say that I blame you. His story was very convincing.'

'I'll tell a man it was,' said Slim flatly. 'There's one thing Kirk Woodward ain't, and that's a liar. And everything fits in. That dead cow, dragged across the line, the butchered steer—'

'Slim!' cried Barbara sharply. 'That'll be enough. Take that—that man outside and see that he receives a decent burial.'

'We'll tote him out, but we shore won't bury him. That's Turner's job. I wouldn't spoil good JKL ground by plantin' his carcass in it. Carry him out the front way, boys, it's shorter.'

They picked up the dead gunman and bore him away, talking among themselves. Ham got to his feet and spoke, his face grave. 'I'll send some men over for the body. I'm honestly glad that Woodward escaped such a horrible death, but of course you won't believe me—now. Good-bye, Miss Lane.'

'Good-bye, Mr. Turner,' said Vivian sweetly. 'Nice to have seen you.'

He went to the door and opened it. 'Wait!' cried Barbara, and hurried after him. They passed to the outside and closed the door after them.

Vivian made a gesture of impatience. 'Why

146

doesn't she let him go? Can't she see that he is simply playing the martyr act? that there isn't a bit of sincerity in him?'

Nellie eyed her wonderingly. 'You mean—you believe Mr. Turner had a hand in it?'

'My dear, I'd believe anything evil of that man. Oh, Nellie! Can't you see that he's all sham and pretense and smooth deceit? You Western girls are so sympathetic and trusting! Let a man appear wearing a linen collar and saying "isn't" instead of "ain't" and you fall to your knees and worship!'

'But Mr. Turner has always been so gentlemanly and polite. Just now, after Kirk had practically accused him and Slim and the boys were ready to believe, he never forgot himself for a moment. He wasn't angry or—or resentful or ready to pull a gun; he just got up quietly and walked out of the room.'

Vivian laughed scornfully. 'My dear little Miss Innocent, when Ham Turner pulls a gun on Kirk Woodward it'll be when Kirk is bound hand and foot and has his back turned. And even then he'll make sure that there's nobody around to see him. As for his leaving so quietly, it was the easiest and quickest way of withdrawing from an embarrassing position. You can see for yourself how it worked; that air of injured innocence pulled Barbara right out after him.'

'But, Vivian—!'

147

Vivian interrupted her shortly. 'Nellie, listen to me. In most things you're a very level-headed young woman, but in this please trust to my judgment. I know Ham Turner's breed; I've associated with men like him all my life. How feeble and insignificant they seem beside your true Western man—straight and honest and clear-eyed and brave!'

'Like Kirk,' murmured Nellie.

'Yes, like Kirk.'

'You admire him, don't you?'

'Admire him! Nellie, I've seen so much more of life than you that I'd come to look upon a man as some sort of predatory beast; but I tell you I could love a man like Kirk Woodward from the depths of my soul!'

Nellie was very grave. 'If you think Mr. Turner's deceiving Barbara you should tell her so.'

'She wouldn't believe me, for all I could tell her is what my instinct tells me. Barbara is disturbingly loyal; she's put Ham Turner on a pedestal because of his suave ways and that superficial education of his. Nothing but the strongest of proof would ever convince her that he's anything less than a paragon. If I were to try to turn her against him I would only hurt her and destroy a friendship I value. No, I can't warn her and you mustn't. She'll see through him some day—or Kirk Woodward'll expose him for what he is. Nellie, you mustn't mention the matter to her.'

Nellie's face tightened. 'If what Kirk accused him of is true, maybe it was he who killed Father!'

Vivian flashed her a keen look. 'Now you're jumping from one extreme to the other. But there were two shots, so perhaps there were two men. If so, you may depend on it Ham fired the one that missed. He's no marksman.'

Beyond the door, Ham had turned in answer to Barbara's summons and was waiting with just the right expression of polite curiosity. He was thinking that he had managed the withdrawal very neatly, for now there was a closed door between them and the annoying Vivian.

'I don't want you to go away angry,' said Barbara anxiously.

'You've chosen the wrong word, my dear. I'm not at all angry—just a little hurt. I had hoped that you might have learned to know me well enough to understand that I couldn't be capable of planning such an outrage or even condoning it. As much as I dislike Woodward, I don't doubt his word. He was far too sincere, and his story rang true. But if he was nailed in that cellar and if the fire was deliberately set to destroy him I must lay the entire responsibility at the door of Depew and Stone. They hated him; Stone's attempt to kill him proves that. If they set that fire they've certainly paid the price. As for Gault, I intend to question him the instant I reach the M, and if he had any part in it I shall pass on to him Woodward's warning and immediately cut him off my payroll.'

Barbara's face lightened. 'I'm glad to hear you say that, Hamilton. I'm ashamed that I doubted you at all.'

His eyes warmed and he impulsively took her hand. 'Thank you, little partner! It's faith like yours that keeps this old world turning.' He released her fingers and drew himself erect. 'And now I'm going to surprise you. Barbara, I've concluded that the cow which was killed and dragged to the Flying W and the steer that was butchered on their land was the work of—the M!'

'The M!' she echoed blankly.

'Perhaps I should say it was the work of somebody employed by the M. It's really very simple after what we've learned. Depew and Stone must have had some kind of a personal feud with Woodward. You'll remember on the night of your party how anxious Depew seemed to kill Woodward. It's my theory now that Depew and Stone killed that cow and butchered the steer in the hope of inflaming the JKL against Kirk Woodward to such an extent that your men would do what I had forbidden them to do for themselves.'

'You mean you had forbidden them to quarrel with Kirk?'

'Not exactly that. I gave them to understand that I didn't want them to force a fight with Woodward. If he started something, then the sky was to be the limit.'

Even Barbara, who wanted to believe him, could not swallow this whole; and realizing it, Ham made a bold attempt to cover up.

'You see,' he said, looking directly at her, 'I learned that at one time you and Kirk were very good friends. Frankly, I didn't want to hurt myself in your estimation by even the thought that I might have contributed to his injury.'

'That was generous of you,' said Barbara quietly. 'Kirk and I were friends; but that was a long time ago and things are quite different now.'

He had weathered the storm. 'Yes, quite different—unfortunately.'

'I'm wondering,' she said steadily, 'if the two shots which were fired at my father were from the rifles of Depew and Stone.'

'I'm afraid we can't blame that on them. The evidence against Tom is too conclusive. He warned your father not to set foot on Flying W range and threatened to shoot him if he did. Your own crew heard him. The prints made by his horse were not over fifty yards from where your father fell. And to clinch the case against him, the boy went into hiding. There's no doubt that Tom Woodward killed Jonathan Lane. Even Kirk had no other theory to advance, and admits that he has no proof that another committed the crime. Asa Woodward or Kirk or one of the homesteaders in their crowd must have set your house afire; nobody else had any motive whatever.'

'It wasn't an accident,' admitted Barbara. 'I distinctly remember smelling kerosene when I was getting ready for bed.'

'Of course it wasn't an accident. Somebody slipped into the house—you never kept the doors locked—and got into the attic. Some kerosene spilled about, a candle to ignite it when it had burned low enough—! I'm sure we can't blame Depew or Stone for that. No, Barbara, the Woodwards are your enemies and must be driven clear off Mustang range before you can know any peace of mind.'

'The Woodwards are hard to drive.'

'Your father would have driven them off, and you reminded me once that you were your father's daughter. Perhaps we've gone about it the wrong way. If I were to make a feint attack on the Flying W, thus drawing all the homesteaders away from their places to the north, why couldn't your crew strike at the Gardner place and work south? We'd have them between us then.'

Barbara frowned thoughtfully. 'My boys have never been anxious to fight the Woodwards; they'll be less anxious now.'

Ham shrugged. 'Very well. It seemed the

152

only plan worth trying. I'll be trotting along now. Good-bye.'

Again she detained him. 'Have you any other suggestion?'

'I'm afraid not. After all, it isn't my war. It wasn't my father who was murdered or my home that was burned. As for the crew, they were hired to take orders from you; if they refuse, you can always hire another bunch.'

'I'll think it over,' she promised.

'Good. Use your own judgment in the matter, and whatever it is, you can count on me to back it to the limit.'

She let him go this time, and he went with the satisfaction of knowing that her belief in him was stronger than ever. He took a circuitous route, for now he was without a bodyguard, and as soon as he arrived at the M he summoned Gault.

'Well,' he said, 'Kirk Woodward is on the loose again.'

Gault started. 'You said *Kirk*. Reckon you mean *Tom*.'

'Not Tom—Kirk. It seems that he's impervious even to fire. He found a shovel and a vegetable cellar and dug his way deep enough to escape the flames. Then he walked into the JKL house, told his story and rode away—after shooting Stoney.'

'He shot Stoney? Right there on the JKL? Good gosh, man, am I hearin' right?'

Ham told him the story and Gault swore

fiercely and feelingly. 'By jacks! that jigger's got to be stopped if it takes every man on the M! He shore ain't bullet-proof!'

'No, and neither are you. Stoney tipped him off that it was you who fired the store and he told me to tell you that he would kill you on sight.'

Gault went white to the lips and for a moment stood staring.

'Well, are you going to let him get away with it?'

'I'm no damned fool,' said Sarge. 'I'm not afraid of a man livin' if I have half a chance, but Kirk Woodward—hell! If he could kill Depew and Stoney in a stand-up fight he could kill me. And if I pot him from the brush I'd be blamed anyhow. Ham, we're in this together. I've done my share; now it's up to yuh to get Woodward while I hunt me a danged tight alibi.'

For a while Ham sat in deep thought, drumming the desk-top with his fingertips. He hated to attempt the removal of Kirk Woodward himself, for physically he was a coward; but Woodward must go, and if Gault refused the job he must do it himself or draw another into the scheme, and this he was determined to avoid. He finally looked up.

'Very well, I'll take care of it. You better ride over to the Box V and keep an eye on Venner. We're stocking him up pretty fast and he's selling as rapidly as he dares. The handling of so much money might give him the idea that he really owns the spread. Any stuff ready to move?'

'No. We're goin' to do some more brandin' tomorrow, and the last bunch ain't healed yet. I'll ride over tonight and lay low until yuh send word that it's safe to come back. How's things going on the JKL?'

'I think I got things straightened out with Barbara all right. Also had a talk with Judge Kelly at the fire. The girl hasn't the slightest idea of the amount she has at her disposal. She's always had all the money she wanted and she doesn't realize how much this rustling has cost Lane. The rebuilding she plans is going to take plenty, but the judge will encourage her in it, of course. We're going to wind up with the JKL in our pocket or I'm a mighty poor prophet.'

'Good! Now I'm gonna get ready to hightail it—and Ham, get that Kirk Woodward and get him good! Yuh hear me? He's too danged smart and he's got to go.'

'He'll go,' promised Ham calmly. 'You can leave it to me.'

★   ★   ★

Meanwhile, Kirk rode as rapidly as he could to the Flying W. He wanted to see his father and relieve his anxiety. As he approached the cabin he saw several horses tied outside, and presently Hank Gardner came to the door, stared unbelievingly and ran back into the house.

They emerged in a bunch as Kirk dismounted—three or four neighbors and Asa Woodward. Kirk's father, too, stared as though he were seeing a ghost.

'Kirk!' he cried chokingly. 'Kirk—it ain't you!'

Kirk grinned and threw an affectionate arm about his shoulders. 'It shore enough is! You cain't down a Woodward; they won't even burn.' Quickly he told them his story.

'Then it *is* the M that's behind all this deviltry!'

'Which means Ham Turner,' said Hank Gardner. 'Kirk, for once he's overplayed his hand. Yuh can put him behind the bars for the rest o' his nat'ral life after that kind of a frame-up.'

Kirk grinned wryly. 'I'm afraid it ain't that easy, Hank. We haven't a bit of proof that Ham had a hand in the deal, and two of the three that might implicate him are gone to their reward. And Gault—well, I sent word to him by Ham that I aimed to see that he joined Stoney and Virg just about half a second after I lay eyes on him. If we can nail *him* and make him talk, we might learn somethin'; otherwise all we can do is wait and watch. Some day Ham'll make his mistake and then we'll have him.'

'Reckon yuh're right,' admitted Hank. 'But, feller, he shore is pilin' up the grief at a lively rate. And don't yuh forget for one minute that he knows how dangerous yuh are. Boy, from here on yuh're shore goin' to have to sprout eyes in the back of yore haid!'

CHAPTER TWELVE

A heavy guard was posted that night, and neighboring homesteaders kept alert for the signal which would call them together. Now that Kirk had returned to fling down the gauntlet at Ham Turner's feet the danger of attack was greater than ever before.

Kirk took his turn riding line, moving slowly back and forth along the western boundary of the Flying W. Once during his vigil he was drawn to the creek bed by the sound of hoofs; but the sound was not one to alarm and he knew even before he reached the fringe of cottonwoods just what to expect. As he sat his saddle in the shadows a column of steers passed along the edge of Barbara's range, descending to the creek bed after the overflow stream had been passed. Before, behind, and on each side rode horsemen who talked in tones which they did not attempt to lower.

Kirk felt anger stir within him. Ever the

theft of cattle was repugnant to him, even though the animals stolen were those of his enemies. These he knew were JKL cows, and the JKL was now the property of Barbara and Nellie Lane. It was bad enough to steal from a hardened cowman like Jonathan; this was robbing orphans. But there was nothing he could do about it. The boys from Bates' Bottom carefully refrained from molesting cattle belonging to the homesteaders, and Rum Blossom had proved a friend in need by sheltering Tom Woodward.

With the evidence against the M steadily accumulating, Kirk could no longer doubt that the Monarch crew were, at the very least, aware of the rustling. There were but two routes the cattle could travel in order to reach the Border: through the small pass in the Mustangs and then south, or directly across the fenced Monarch range. Heretofore he had been inclined to believe that the pass had been used; now, knowing Ham Turner for what he was, Kirk was certain the cattle were being driven across the M range.

It was barely possible that Ham knew nothing of this. He was a tenderfoot and not given to riding abroad at night, and his crew, chosen mostly from the population of Bates' Bottom, might easily be gathering a little velvet on the side; but Kirk was not willing to give Turner the benefit of the doubt. The man was grasping, unscrupulous, and had shown himself a master of hypocrisy.

The cattle passed, and presently a band of horsemen came loping up the creek bed to obliterate the tracks as much as possible. At the point where the cattle had been driven into the creek bed they turned and rode away towards the M, and Kirk recognized the voices of Shab Townsend and Joel Cord.

Kirk was unusually glum when he turned in after being relieved. Every honest instinct urged him to get word to Slim Chance so that the JKL crew could be on guard. Their cattle roamed far and the loss they were suffering could not even be estimated until fall round-up when the cattle were gathered and tallied. They knew and expected the loss of an occasional steer to a meat-hungry homesteader, but certainly none of them dreamed that the critters were going a hundred or more at a time. But, despite his aversion to the whole thing, Kirk knew that he could not warn Slim, for the fact remained that were it not for Rum Blossom Bates his brother Tom would now be a prisoner of Jake Benson awaiting trial for the murder of Jonathan Lane.

His father spoke to him over the breakfast table. 'Son, we got to get to work buildin' a new barn and wagon shed. Yuh reckon we can get some lumber from the mill at Mustang?'

'Don't see why not. It belongs to the

Lanes, but so does the store. They cain't refuse to sell from one any more than from the other.'

'Then we better drive in and get us some.'

'I can do it. Nobody's goin' to start anything in broad daylight, and things have changed a heap since the other night.'

'Daylight or dark, it ain't safe for either of us to travel alone.'

'I reckon it's worth chancin' this once. It's a waste of time for both of us to go, when you could be gettin' out some logs for the foundation. No place along that upper road for them to ambush me, and I'm shore not afraid of them tacklin' me in town. Even Ham Turner wouldn't have the gall to try that.'

So immediately after breakfast he hitched up and started for Mustang. One of Jonathan Lane's sidelines had been the operation of a small sawmill under the direction of a man named Hopper. At the lumber yard in town there was kept available at all times a supply of rough lumber which Kirk knew would serve their purpose.

He nodded grimly at his father's admonition to 'Take keer of yoreself,' and headed north. At Gardner's homestead he turned into the upper road, for although he felt that Slim and his boys were more favorably disposed towards him since his narrow escape, he had no intention of

160

ignoring the warning to stay off the JKL trail.

Men stared at him as he drove along the street and not a few of them called to him or waved friendly greetings. There is always sympathy for the underdog, especially if he happens unexpectedly to emerge on top; and while most of the townsmen favored the cattleman as against the nester, the attempt on Kirk's life had been a bit too raw for them to stomach. As he climbed out of the wagon before the little shack which Hopper used as an office, he noticed the two horses which stood at the rail outside Judge Kelly's home and knew that Barbara and Ham Turner were in town. He went inside to purchase his lumber.

In the judge's living room, Barbara and Ham were about to take their leave. They had called to arrange certain details concerning the rebuilding of the business block which had been destroyed by fire.

'It's settled, then, that we use brick,' said the judge. 'As I told you, it will be much more expensive, but the danger of another costly fire will be greatly lessened and the block will improve the whole appearance of our little town.' He smiled benignly on the girl. 'Your father loved this humble little village; I'm sure he'd want it to be just as attractive as we can make it.'

'Of course,' said Barbara. 'By all means use brick.'

'We'll need quite a bit of lumber, too, both in the construction here and for your new home. It might be wise to ask Hopper to hold on to the stock he has on hand. We want to get the job of building through as quickly as possible and we don't want any shortages.'

So, after bidding him good morning, Barbara and Ham started across the street towards Hopper's office, and if they noticed the wagon standing in front of it, neither recognized it as belonging to the Flying W. Hopper had greeted Kirk pleasantly and reckoned he had just what the Woodwards needed. He made out a sales slip, noting the footage and the price, and Kirk pocketed it and paid him. Then as he turned to leave, the door opened and Barbara and Turner entered.

He touched the brim of his hat, but Barbara looked directly at Hopper, ignoring Kirk. 'I stopped in, Mr. Hopper, to tell you not to release another foot of lumber without first seeing me. We're going to do a lot of building and we'll need every bit we have on hand.'

'Why, shore, Miss Barbara. I just sold Kirk, here, a little of that rough stuff—'

'I'm afraid you'll have to cancel the sale. We'll need the rough lumber for scaffolding.'

Hopper looked at Kirk and got a solemn nod. 'Go ahead and tell her, Hop. The lumber's already bought and paid for.'

She spoke to the embarrassed clerk. 'Give Mr. Woodward his money.'

'Uh—yes'm.' Hopper pushed the money on the counter towards Kirk.

'It's not my money,' said Kirk. 'I just swapped it for boards.'

Barbara turned to him then, a flush of anger on her cheeks. 'The lumber is the property of the JKL. I'm one of the owners, in case you don't know, and I'm trying to tell you in a nice way that we have no lumber for sale.'

'That's quite all right with me, Miss Lane,' said Kirk formally. 'I don't need any more; what I just bought will rebuild part of what the JKL burned down.'

Turner interrupted. 'I don't see how Miss Lane can make it any plainer, Woodward. There's your money—take it. The sale is off.'

Kirk's eyes hardened. 'I thought you'd have to put yore yap in it before we got through. Now listen to me, Ham Turner. This is a lumber yard with a man in charge who's paid for sellin' lumber. I told him what I wanted and he made me a price. I paid, and hold a receipted sales slip to show for it. That constitutes an iron-clad contract that cain't be broke by no tenderfoot named Ham Turner or no imitation society lady named Barbara Lane. It's my lumber and I'm goin' out and round it up right now.'

Barbara stepped in front of him, lips tight,

eyes flashing. 'Kirk Woodward, I dare you to lay a hand on a board of ours!'

He smiled down on her a bit grimly. 'Barbara, you should remember from other days that when you *dared* me to do a thing that was just the time I did it.' He moved a step to his right, intending to pass her, but she moved with him, her defiant gaze still upon him.

Swiftly and surely he reached out and gripped her by both arms at the elbows, and before she knew what he was about he had raised her from the floor and thrust her into Turner's arms. 'Here, Ham, you hold her. I got work to do.'

Ham automatically put his arms about the angry girl, only to drop her hastily at her furious, 'Put me down!' By that time Kirk was at the door and she saw the amused grin on his face as he closed it after him.

He drove into the yard, and while he was stacking the boards in the wagon had a fleeting glimpse of Ham hurrying across the street. When he drove out with his load it was to see Ham returning with Sheriff Benson. The latter stepped in front of the horses and halted them.

'Hold up!' he ordered. 'Where yuh think yuh're goin'?'

'To the Flyin' W, of course,' answered Kirk mildly.

'Not with that lumber, yuh ain't. Yuh was

told it ain't for sale. Turn 'round and drive back into the yard.'

'Now wait a minute! This lumber's mine; I bought it before Hopper was told to clamp the lid on.'

'I don't give a dang about that. Turn 'round and drive back into the yard and unload.'

'But I tell you—!'

'Yuh've told me enough, feller! I'm gettin' tired of yuh nesters goin' 'round tellin' folks; it's time somebody got yuh told off. Right now yuh oughta be under lock and key for aidin' and abettin' that killer brother of yores!'

'Jake, the lumber is mine. I have a slip to show for it. Look here.' He reached inside his coat with the evident intention of getting the sales slip, but before Jake could realize that he was reaching with the wrong hand and on the wrong side the double-barreled Derringer was out and pointing squarely at Turner.

There was a harsh ring to Kirk's voice as he spoke now. 'Listen, you little two-bit lawman! I got Old Faithful pointed square at Ham Turner and if you make a move towards yore gun my thumb is shore as hell goin' to slip off the hammer. I'm aimin' at him instead of you because much as I don't like you, I don't like him a lot more.' He heard Barbara exclaim from some point behind him, and answered without turning his head. 'And

165

as for you, little imitation society lady, don't you go startin' anything or yore Ham is shore enough goin' to be cooked.'

'Yuh're under arrest for resistin' an officer!' cried Benson furiously.

'You forgot to add "in the performance of his duty." You ain't performin' the duty of an officer in tryin' to prevent a man movin' his lawful property. Ham, get up on this seat with me. I aim to take you along as security.'

Ham glanced at the sheriff, then back again. 'I shall do nothing—'

'You'll climb into this wagon before I count three or I'll shoot a leg out from under you!'

Ham was in the seat at the count of two.

'Now take up those reins and drive, so's I can keep this persuader against yore short ribs. Jake, you try to pot-shot me and Ham shore gets his. Go on, Ham—start drivin'.'

Ham drove, face tight with anger. At the edge of town Kirk looked back. The sheriff and the group which had been attracted by the argument still stood in the same place. He ordered Ham to halt and dismount. When he started the team, he saw Jake Benson running towards his office. Kirk urged the horses to a gallop and looped the reins about the brake lever. Fishing his Winchester from the wagon bed, he got on his knees and rested his elbows on the seat.

Jake came riding around the end building and Kirk aimed deliberately and fired. The sheriff reined in at once. 'Reckon that'll hold him,' murmured Kirk. 'Shot for his hat, but was scared I'd plug him and held a bit too high.'

Ham Turner strode back to where he had left Barbara, Benson riding beside him and explaining how completely handcuffed he had been. Ham did not reply. His face was still white and he was shaking with anger.

'He got away with it again,' he told Barbara bitterly. 'Always he manages to make me look ridiculous in your eyes.'

'If ever I have the chance,' she said tightly, 'I'll punish him as he has never been punished before.'

Ham rode home with her, then continued on to the Monarch, taking a route which would miss the Flying W. He found the M ranch yard deserted and the only sound he could detect was that of snoring. He left his horse and quietly walked to the cook shanty and looked in. The cook was sleeping on his bunk, and an empty whiskey bottle stood on the table. Ham nodded his satisfaction and continued to the house.

This was his chance and he suddenly determined to take it. He had promised Sarge Gault to rid the world of Kirk Woodward, but he had made the promise with his fingers crossed; now his humiliation at the hands of the fellow crystalized mere desire into earnest resolve. He would kill Kirk Woodward, but he would do it in such a way that the deed could never be traced to him.

He went into Gault's room and donned a pair of his overalls and also some cast-off boots of the foreman. From his own room he took a Winchester rifle and a pair of binoculars in a leather case. Going to the cook's shanty, he listened to be sure that the fellow still slept, then mounted his horse and rode away. He followed the road which led to the pass, turning presently into a trail which he had ridden once before with murder in his heart. At the south fence of the Flying W he halted and dismounted. Tying the horse securely, he squirmed through the wire.

The fringe of brush and trees protected him. He scrambled down the bank of the overflow stream and leaped across the water. He left two excellent prints, but made no effort to erase them. Nobody would associate tracks so large with Hamilton Turner. A low bush grew on the lip of the opposite bank, and to this Ham crawled, there to peer through the foliage at the Woodward cabin.

Two men were building a shed. The uprights were in place and now they were putting on the siding. Occasionally one or the other would pass out of sight behind the cabin, to return with a board balanced on his shoulder. Ham got out the binoculars and focused them. He could see distinctly now. Both men were in their shirtsleeves, but Kirk was wearing his hat and his father was bareheaded.

Ham placed the binoculars on the ground and shoved the rifle through the bush. He was shaking and his heart beat irregularly. Steady, he told himself; there must be no mistake. He sighted the rifle at the man with the hat, followed his every step to the cabin, picked him up again as he reappeared with a plank. Three times he did this, until he was absolutely certain of his aim. His nerves quieted and he followed his target unerringly.

Father and son were working together now; they finished nailing a board in place and disappeared behind the cabin. The next time the man with the hat emerged, he would kill him. Ham braced his elbows firmly and squinted along the barrel of the Winchester. The end of a plank appeared and he took up the trigger slack. Had to be sure it was the man wearing the hat. It was!

The rifle cracked and Ham, watching avidly, saw the figure stop in midstride; then the plank fell from the fellow's shoulder, he staggered blindly for a pace or two, then collapsed on the ground.

Ham scurried down the bank and ran as fast as he could. A wild panic gripped him; he ran in great leaps, springing across the stream, struggling up the bank, crashing through the brush to the fence. Not until he was in the saddle did he gain some measure of composure. He was filled with fear, but beneath that emotion he felt a great satisfaction. The deed was done; Kirk Woodward was no more!

CHAPTER THIRTEEN

By the time he reached the M headquarters, Ham had conquered his panic. There had been no pursuit and he had returned by such devious ways that he was sure he could not be followed. The cook still slept; nobody could testify to his going and coming. He stripped his horse and went into the house where he changed from Gault's overalls and boots to his own riding breeches and footwear. That accomplished, he felt secure.

A feeling of pride in achievement filled him; he had destroyed the Big Bad Wolf—had succeeded where all others had failed. It did not occur to him that the victory was in reality Gault's, that it was Sarge who had first suggested ambush as the safest and most certain way of removing a troublesome and dangerous enemy. Forgotten, too, was the fact that the schemes which had failed were the product of his own masterly mind.

That mind was already busy with plans to end forever the resistance of the homesteaders. With Kirk Woodward out of the way the time to strike was now; if the JKL would not help he would manage without them. He saddled a fresh horse and set out for Mustang pass and the Box V. It was shortly past noon when he pulled up at Venner's place, to find the horsefaced man and Gault at the dinner table. They had just finished their meal and he came to the point at once.

'Cliff, have your men saddle up and ride over to the M. We're going to finish off the nesters tonight once and for all.'

Venner stared at him doubtfully. 'Kinda risky draggin' us into somethin' on the other side of the range, ain't it?'

'You heard my order,' said Ham coldly, and Venner went outside. Ham addressed Gault in what he hoped was a casual tone. 'Well, I got Kirk Woodward.'

Sarge nearly fell out of his chair. 'Yuh got Kirk Woodward!'

'Of course.' Ham eyed him quizzically. 'I said I would, didn't I?'

'Yeah, but—! Holy cow, Ham, how'd yuh do it?'

Ham told him, not mentioning the use of Gault's overalls and boots. 'I can't be positive that I killed him, but I knocked him off his feet and if he isn't dead we can finish him tonight.'

Sarge lost some of his enthusiasm. 'Oh! Yuh ain't shore, then.'

'Not any more so than when you shot Lane. He dropped, just like Lane dropped, and he didn't get up.'

Gault shook his head. 'Jest the same I'm layin' low until yuh're shore. Venner can testify that I ain't been off this range. They cain't blame the shootin' on me.'

Ham helped himself to what was left on the table, and presently Venner came in with the report that his men would start within the hour. Ham left at once, reaching home by mid-afternoon. He strode into the living room and halted as abruptly as though a stone wall had suddenly erected itself before him. Kirk Woodward spoke grimly.

'Come in and sit down, Ham. I want to powwow with you.'

A chill of apprehension ran through Ham's blood and he felt as though a hand had gripped him by the throat. He had made a mistake after all! He had failed miserably as had the others! Forcing his numbed muscles to respond, he crossed to a chair and sat down.

'Where's Gault?' asked Kirk.

'I don't know. I discharged him for his part in that fire.'

'Yeah, you did! Come on—where is he?'

'I'm telling you the truth. And I gave him your message before he left.'

'I still think you're lyin'. Reckon it's news to you that he shot my father this mornin'.'

172

'Your father!' Ham's surprise was genuine.

'Yes. Shot him from the same bunch of brush that I reckon he hid in when he shot Jonathan Lane. I figure he was after me. Dad was bareheaded and I wasn't, but just before he was shot he put his hat on and Gault likely mistook him for me.'

'Was your father—killed?'

'No, bullet smashed his shoulder. Too bad, ain't it?'

'Yes—I mean, no! Confound it! Are you trying to make me say I'm sorry he wasn't killed? How do you know Gault did it?'

'By the tracks he left at the water hole. Looked around and found his boots upstairs. The fresh mud is still on them. Where were you this mornin'?'

There was only one way out for Ham and he took it. 'I was on the other side of the hills talking cattle with a rancher named Venner. Gault must have sneaked into the house while I was gone.'

Kirk got up. 'I thought you and him might be together on the deal. I still *think* you were, but right now I got nothin' on you; but if I catch you with him I'll *know* and I'll kill you both.'

He stalked from the room and Ham, watching from a window, saw him get his horse from behind the house and ride away. Turner was still shaken; he had been so sure, had taken every precaution, and still the man lived to defy him. The night's job would be rendered more difficult now, but he had to go through with it. From here on it would be either himself or Kirk Woodward all the way down the line. After a while he went outside, got on his horse and rode to Mustang. Here he had a long talk with Jake Benson, after which the sheriff spent some time selecting a posse.

Kirk rode home by way of Bates' Bottom, stopping there in the hope of finding Gault; but all the able-bodied inhabitants were across the Line with JKL beef. He talked with Tom, acquainting him with what had happened, but minimizing the injury to their father, then rode on to the Flying W. There he found a bunch of angry homesteaders. This shooting from ambush had stirred them deeply, and with the coming of darkness a heavier than usual guard was set.

Kirk was eating supper when the cabin door opened softly and a man entered. He whirled about to see Tom. The boy explained shortly.

'I had to see Dad. Couldn't stay cooped up in the Bottom knowin' he was hurt.' He went over to the bunk and took the lax hand which lay outside the cover. 'How you makin' it, old timer?'

'All right,' came the feeble response. 'But yuh—hadn't oughta—come. If they lay their hands on yuh—'

'I'm goin' right back. I hate to, but I reckon it's best.'

A volley of rifle fire rang out along the south boundary, and he sprang to his feet.

'Come along,' said Kirk and led the way outside.

A rider approached them at a thundering gallop while from a nearby point a pile of brush burst into flame. The horseman drew up at Kirk's challenge and reported tersely, 'The M! They're cutting yore south wire.'

'Get back there and help hold 'em. Tom, you better cut through the hills to the Bottom while you got the chance.'

'I'll stick around a while. No use runnin' till I have to.'

Kirk did not have the heart to deny him. He saddled up and the two of them rode to the south boundary from whence came the steady crack of rifles and the boom of six guns. Will Gardner came to meet them.

'Kirk? Gosh a'mighty, man! They've busted through the fence at half a dozen places. Mebbe we can hold them on the other side of the creek if we can get these fires started.'

They worked swiftly, piling brush and firing it. Once the south line was illuminated and the men posted there could shoot with no more certainty, Kirk and Tom rode to the west line where they found Hank and Sam Gardner also busy stacking and firing brush in anticipation of an attack by the JKL.

Homesteaders began to arrive in answer to the signal, and Kirk posted them in advantageous positions. The firing continued along the south border, but investigation showed that the M crew had not attempted to cross the creek. Thus far there was no sign of activity on the JKL.

'I reckon we stopped them just in time,' said Kirk. 'Tom, you better—'

He broke off, stiffening in the saddle. From some point far to the north of them had come the sound of scattered gunfire.

Hank Gardner came riding up. 'Yuh hear that, Kirk? It's up on my place. What yuh figger is goin' on?'

The reports continued, gradually growing louder. Gardner paced his horse back and forth, his apprehension mounting. Will rode over from the south boundary to join him, and a number of other homesteaders left their posts, all concerned for the safety of the women and children they had left behind them.

Then a horse came lunging out of the darkness and a frightened boy shouted to them from its back. 'They's a whole gang of men ridin' this way and drivin' everybody in front of 'em! They're bustin' windows and pullin' down sheds and shootin' our stock! The crops are all trampled and the fences are down!'

A chorus of angry exclamations came from the assembled homesteaders, and almost as one man they started towards the north as rapidly as their horses could carry them.

'Kirk, I gotta leave yuh,' said Hank agitatedly. 'Hate to do it, but my wife and little kids are back there. Come on, boys, let's ride!'

He left with his sons at a high lope, and Kirk wouldn't have stopped them if he could. It was useless to warn them that they were inviting defeat by dividing their forces; no father or brother could be expected to defend another man's home when his own was in danger.

Shouts from the south line told Kirk that the M was making a charge, and he hastily gathered what few men he had left to repulse it. Turner's crew had crossed the stream and were firing from the protection of the bank.

For an hour the little band of defenders fought savagely to hold them in check, and when they were finally driven from the stream Kirk turned to meet a motley collection of spring wagons and buckboards which came bouncing across the Flying W range. They contained women and children, frightened and crying. Behind them, forming a protecting screen, were the mounted homesteaders.

'They's a hull flock of fellers follerin' us,' reported Hank Gardner. 'Don't know who they are, but they're bustin' everything in their way. Tried to hold 'em, but there's too many. Kirk, we're licked this time.'

Kirk thought swiftly. There was no time to gather brush and start fresh fires along the north boundary, and if he sent his men against this strange band approaching from that direction, the M outfit would take them in the rear. And now there were women and children to consider.

'Only one thing to do,' he said. 'Hank, I'm dependin' on you and the rest of the boys to keep yore heads. We've got to get back in the hills to that line shack of ours. There we can stand them off. We'll put Dad in one of the wagons. Keep together, with the men on the outside. Hank, you take charge; I'll join you in a few minutes.'

Ordering Tom to accompany him, he rode swiftly to the creek bed on the edge of the JKL range. 'Cut across the JKL and circle behind the Monarch crowd,' he said. 'That way you can make it to the Bottom.'

'I'm not leavin' you now,' said Tom stubbornly.

'Listen, Tom. You know the shape Dad's in. If they get you it'll finish him. One rifle more or less won't matter now. Get out while you can.'

For a moment longer Tom sat there, but the logic of Kirk's appeal could not be denied and finally he swore bitterly and spurred across the creek bed to the JKL range. And almost instantly came the sound of a challenge followed by the crack of a rifle. Kirk heard the tramping of hoofs and a yell of triumph in the voice of Jake Benson.

'It's Tom Woodward! I got his hoss! Nail him, boys!'

Another shot rang out as Kirk kicked his horse down the bank and up the opposite side. By the faint light of the fires he saw Tom on his feet beside his dead horse, saw a half-circle of horsemen closing in. He thumbed his six-gun, aiming low, and two horses went down under his lead; then he was on his feet beside Tom. The boy was staggering, trying to keep erect.

'I'm hit!' he groaned. 'Kirk, get outa here!'

Kirk pivoted his horse, clinging to the bit with one hand. With the other he literally threw Tom astride the animal. 'Hang on, kid! Ride for the line shack. Go on—*ride!*' A smack on the rump sent the horse bounding towards the Flying W.

He whirled. Benson's men were all about him; their forms towered over him. Lead whipped at his clothing, then the shoulder of a horse struck him and sent him sprawling. He rolled away from the churning hoofs but men flung themselves from their saddles and piled on him. A vicious blow on the head knocked him out.

He was unconscious for only a short time,

but when he recovered his hands were cuffed behind him and Jake Benson was berating him.

'I wisht I'd hit yuh harder and put yuh where yuh belong! But as it is yuh'll shore pay plenty for this. We had that murderin' brother of yores dead to rights. Yuh'll get ten years for interferin' with the law . . . Skinny, take two men and rustle some hosses. I'm not walkin' back to Mustang.'

Three of the posse started away in search of mounts and the rest sprawled on the ground. Kirk's heart was sore within him. Off to the east he could hear the bark of rifles and the thunder of six-guns as the little band of fugitive homesteaders fought their way to the hills. Among them, he hoped, was Tom.

For hours they lay there waiting. Dawn came—a dawn that looked on shattered houses, ruined crops and tumbled and snarled wire fence. Presently the three came up with as many extra horses; saddles were rigged and Kirk was pushed astride one of them. Benson flipped a noose over his head and drew it tight. The whole party set out for the JKL.

As they rode into the yard the girls came from the house and the JKL crew from their bunkhouse. Kirk knew then that Barbara's men had taken no part in the attack. Somewhere Ham had collected another crew.

Benson swung to the ground. 'Light, boys, and stretch yore legs. Mawnin', ladies.

Reckon yuh could scare up some grub for us?'

'I'll tell the cook,' said Barbara in a smothered voice.

Vivian approached Benson, her eyes flashing with anger. 'What are you doing with Mr. Woodward?'

'Takin' him to jail, ma'am. He's shore a bad actor. We had that killer brother of his'n all rounded up and he had to bu'st in and get him away from us. I socked him with my gun bar'l and messed up that hard head of his'n.'

'Take that rope from about his neck! Do you think he's a dog?'

'I think he's a right slippery customer. That rope stays.'

'If you don't take that rope off him, Jake Benson, I'll go the Governor in person and prefer charges against you! Mr. Woodward has been hurt and I intend to dress the wound.'

Benson gave a surly order and Kirk was lifted from the saddle and the rope and handcuffs removed. Nellie, at a word from Vivian, went into the house for water and bandages, and Kirk, also at her direction, sat down on the gallery steps. Nellie, white-faced and shaken, returned with cloth and water. 'Tom?' she whispered. 'He's all right?'

'I got him on my hoss and headed him for that old line shack of ours,' he answered in a low voice. 'He was shot, but was still on his feet. I reckon he made it.'

'Shot!' gasped Nellie. 'Dear God!' She went quickly into the house.

Kirk spoke to Slim Chance who, with the JKL boys, stood watching in grim silence. 'Slim, I owe you and the boys an apology. When that bunch started drivin' out the women and children I thought it was you.'

'We ain't that lowdown,' growled Chance.

'I know it. And somethin' else happened that you might want to know. This mornin' my father was shot from ambush.'

'Oh, no!' cried Vivian in a shocked voice.

'Yes. The feller was layin' in the same clump of brush where Tom claims the one who shot Jonathan Lane was hid. I aim to find him, and when I do I reckon we'll know who really killed Lane.'

Vivian finished bandaging his wound and got him something to eat. The posse hastily downed the food which was passed among them and had just finished the meal when a triumphant Ham Turner rode into the yard with his outfit. Barbara had come outside, and Ham addressed her with a beaming face.

'Well, we fixed them this time! Chased them into the hills and ruined everything they left behind. I don't believe you'll be troubled with nesters in the future.'

Kirk looked up at Barbara, his lips twisted. 'Who's the cad now?'

She started and her eyes blazed but she did

182

not answer. Ham, however, turned on him furiously. 'I'll take no lip from you, Woodward! Aiding and abetting in the escape of a murderer is a serious offense, and I'll use every bit of influence I possess to see that you serve a long prison term for it.'

Kirk got to his feet and stared up at the man. 'And now you listen to me, you hirer of thugs and killers! You're proud of what you've done; you think you're sittin' on top of the world. Well, I'm not licked yet, and in the end I'm goin' to send you where you belong! Now you can charge me with threat to kill and add some more years to that stretch.'

Ham's face purpled and he swung to the ground.

'Go ahead and strike him,' said Vivian bitterly. 'You have enough men to back you up.'

'Hell, he ain't got the guts!' blurted Slim Chance.

'Slim!' cried Barbara sharply. 'That was uncalled for.'

He eyed her coldly. 'I've been honin' to tell him that for weeks. Me and the boys are all for the JKL, and as long as yore pa was livin' we were ready to fight for the spread at the drop of a hat; but now Jonathan's gone and this tenderfoot keeps hornin' in where he don't belong. There was no trouble until he come here, and yore pa, hatin' nesters as he

183

did, would shore draw the line at turnin' women and children out of their homes.'

'Who was it burned the JKL house over the heads of three sleeping women?' cried Ham.

'I'll bite,' said Slim. 'Who was it?'

'Woodward's bunch, of course! Who else?'

'That's what me and the boys been wonderin'. You see, we cain't figger out how somebody we knew is an enemy of the outfit ever got into that house without bein' seen goin' or comin'.'

'What are you insinuating?' demanded Ham fiercely.

'I ain't 'sinuatin' nothin'; I'm makin' the plain statement that I believe somebody set that fire a-purpose so that the Woodwards would be blamed.'

Turner almost choked. 'You're crazy! Crazy as a loon!'

'Not as crazy as yuh wished I was, Turner. If yuh ask me, I think Sarge Gault set that fire. He was over here that evenin'—and you were with him. And a foreman usually does things to order!'

'Slim!' cried Barbara. 'You apologize to Mr. Turner for that!'

But the honest Slim was entirely out of hand. 'Apologize? To him? I'd as soon apologize to a diamond-back rattler!'

Barbara's face was tight. 'Slim, you'll take that back or—'

'Yes'm?'

'—or you can get your time!'

For a moment Slim regarded her steadily. 'So I'm fired, huh? Well, I'm sorry. I've worked a right smart spell for the JKL, and I reckon I always did my best; but lately they's been too many raw deals pulled on this man's range to let me sleep comfortable nights.' He turned abruptly and strode towards the bunkhouse, and the rest of the crew, after exchanging understanding glances, followed him.

'Good riddance,' said Benson. 'Cinch up, boys, and we'll be on our way.'

While they were working with their rigs, Nellie came from the house dressed for riding. Without a word to any of them she started for the corral, but Barbara called after her. 'Nellie, where are you going?'

She turned, her small white face set determinedly. 'Tom's hurt. I'm going to find him and take care of him, and I don't care what you think!' She hurried on to the corral. Barbara stared after her, cheeks burning, her lips compressed into a fine line.

Kirk spoke bitterly. 'Take a good look at her, Barbara. She's worth it. All wool and a yard wide, just like her sister—used to be!'

Before she could think of an answer he turned, thanked Vivian quietly and climbed into the saddle. Again his hands were cuffed, and the little party started for Mustang.

Kirk rode erect and defiant, although his heart was dead. The homesteaders were broken, their homes and crops and stock destroyed. His father, dangerously hurt, was dependent upon the care of neighbors, and Tom, wounded and hunted, must hole up like a wild beast to lick his injuries. Kirk himself was certain of his fate; he would be persecuted by those in power and the very least he could expect was a long term of imprisonment. There was not the slightest ray of hope. He was licked. Despite his brave defiance of Ham Turner he was absolutely and utterly licked.

CHAPTER FOURTEEN

Barbara stood at the window watching the little body of men who rode towards Mustang. Ham Turner had left at the same time as had the sheriff and now she saw that he had joined the latter's party. Her gaze, however, was not on him; she was watching an erect form with bound hands and a white bandage beneath his Stetson: Kirk Woodward.

There was a feeling of dismay within her, a feeling which she tried to subdue and couldn't. She told herself sternly that she should be glad that at last this man who had taunted her and scorned her and insulted her was on his way to prison, but she knew that she wasn't glad. Instead, the thought of Kirk Woodward confined behind stout walls stirred a deep pity. Prison would break him. Either that or instill within him a hatred for the men who had put him there, which, when finally unleashed, would surely bring his destruction.

Further to disturb her was the knowledge that she might possibly be mistaken about the Woodwards. She knew that the JKL was losing some stock, and Ham Turner had assured her that the loss was caused by the nesters on the far side of the creek. She had been quite confident that these same nesters were responsible for the ranch house fire, and certainly the evidence that Tom Woodward had killed her father was as conclusive as it could be.

Yet to her anger and dismay, doubt had crept into the minds of those upon whom she had depended. Vivian Stacy openly scorned the idea that Tom had shot Jonathan Lane, and her own sister Nellie had gone out to search for Tom and minister to his wound. Slim Chance, of all men, had bluntly stated the belief of the crew that the ranch house fire had been set by Sarge Gault in order that Kirk Woodward would be blamed for it. He had even gone so far as to imply that Hamilton Turner had been behind the thing, and for that she had been forced to discharge him. Surely, she told herself, Slim would regret his heated words and ask to be reinstated.

But Slim did no such thing. She heard the clump of boots on the gallery and turned from the window to see Slim, Eaglebeak Smitty, Tex Evans, and Sam and Chuck Brady standing in the doorway. She nodded to them and Slim spoke soberly.

'Miss Barbara, we come to tell yuh to get yoreself another crew. I argued with these jugheads but they wouldn't listen to me. They aim to quit too.'

She hid her panic beneath a mask of hardness. 'You've made up your minds?'

'Shore have,' drawled Tex. 'We ain't seein' Slim back down to nobody like Ham Turner. There ain't nothin' else to do unless yuh figger it ain't noways necessary for him to apologize.'

Barbara's lips tightened. 'Very well, I'll ride to Mustang and ask Judge Kelly to find another crew. I'll pay you off this evening.'

They shuffled away and she went to the bedroom to change her clothes. Vivian was already dressed in riding togs and she told the Eastern girl of her intentions.

'I'm going to town myself,' said Vivian. 'If you like we can ride together.'

There was a moment's silence between them, then Barbara put much the same question as had her sister Nellie. 'You believe in Kirk Woodward, don't you?'

The answer was emphatic. 'Absolutely. I believe him to be a much wronged man.'

'It seems that everybody is beginning to believe in him,' said Barbara bitterly, 'except Mr. Turner and myself.'

'And if you'll admit it, Barbara, your lack of belief is due mostly to Mr. Turner. Well, Ham Turner could be wrong; you'd better climb on the bandwagon with the rest of us.'

'And make friends with Kirk Woodward?' Barbara was astonished. 'How can you suggest such a thing! Even if Tom were innocent of Father's death, even if they had no knowledge of the fire, Kirk Woodward has humiliated me and insulted me and I've promised that I'd drive him from Mustang range if it was the last thing I ever do.'

'Well, at the moment it appears as though Ham Turner had accomplished that for you. Let's talk of brighter things. What are you going to wear?'

When they reached Mustang they saw a number of horses tied before the judge's office and knew that he must be here instead of at his home. They dismounted and went inside. At the far end of the room sat Kelly, red-faced and pompous. At the desk beside him was Ham Turner, and Benson and his prisoner stood before them. As the girls hesitated in the doorway they heard the

189

judge's heavy voice.

'Do you mean to tell me, Kirk Woodward, that you plead not guilty to the charge of aiding a criminal to escape the law?'

'That's right, Judge. I helped Tom get away, yes; but since he didn't kill Jonathan Lane he's no criminal.'

'Whether or not he is guilty is for a jury to decide. As it is, Tom Woodward is charged with the crime and you must answer to the law for helping him. I am fixing the amount of your bail at ten thousand dollars.'

'You know I can never post that amount.'

Ham Turner sneered across the desk. 'Of course we know it. You don't think we're going to have you running around loose, do you? Take him away and lock him up, Benson.'

'Just a moment, please!' Vivian moved forward quickly and for the first time Turner and Kelly saw the girls. 'How do you do, Judge? May I borrow your pen for a moment?'

The judge got to his feet with a bow which he intended to seem courtly.

'Ah! Miss Stacy, you honor my poor court with your presence. Most certainly you may use my pen.' He dipped the instrument in question in the ink and tendered it to her.

She gave him a saccharin smile. 'Thank you so much. You said the amount of the bail is ten thousand dollars, didn't you? Shall I

190

make my check payable to you personally?'

From her bag she produced a checkbook, and now held the pen poised over one of the blanks.

'Vivian!' cried Kirk protestingly.

'You're about to furnish bail for him?' asked Ham Turner angrily. 'Now see here, Miss Stacy, I can't allow you—'

'Of course you can't,' interrupted Vivian. 'You have nothing whatever to do with it. To you personally, Judge?'

Kelly was uncomfortable, but not so much so that he couldn't see the advantage of having the check payable to him in the event Kirk decided to jump his bail. 'Uh—yes, to me personally, if you please.'

'Vivian, you mustn't do this!' cried Kirk desperately.

'Nonsense. The money will be refunded when you appear for trial ... There you are, Judge. Mr. Woodward is free now, isn't he?'

'Uh—yes. Just as soon as you sign a few blanks. Matter of form, you know. I'll prepare them for you at once.'

Ham came around the desk, his face dark. For once he forgot to be his polite self. 'Are you crazy?' he asked in a low voice. 'He'll jump his bail as sure as I'm a foot high!'

'How nice!' she murmured. 'Would you get the whole ten thousand, or would you have to split with the judge?' She turned her back and he walked over to the astonished and angry Barbara.

'I hope you had no hand in this. With Kirk Woodward in a cell we could settle with these nesters and get our hands on the murderer of your father. Now she's spoiled it all.'

'Of course I had nothing to do with it. I can't understand what Vivian is about.' She turned stormy eyes on the Eastern girl who, having signed the papers, was approaching with Kirk. Woodward, stiff and uncompromising, continued to the doorway; Vivian halted before Barbara and spoke quietly.

'I'm sorry if I've offended you, dear. I just had to do it. I won't embarrass you by returning to the ranch. If you'll send my things to the hotel I'll be ever so grateful. Good-bye, dear, and try not to think too unkindly of me.'

She joined Kirk at the doorway and then they went outside together. On the sidewalk he turned to her resentfully. 'Vivian, I won't be indebted to you for such an amount. You make me feel—cheap.'

'You mustn't be silly, Kirk. I'm glad that I'm in a position to do this for you, and as I said, it will be returned to me. I'm thinking of your father and Tom; they need you. Now run along, and if you ever hit Ham Turner again, hit him extra hard for me!'

She mounted her pony and rode away without glancing back. As he moved to his own horse, he saw Barbara come out in the company of Ham and Benson. The men were talking in low tones and stared at him malignantly. He mounted and set out for the Flying W.

At first he rode slowly, thoughts on this beautiful Eastern girl who had come so whole-heartedly to his assistance. The red stained his cheeks as he reviewed the affair in his mind, for with the pride of his sex he considered it a matter for shame to be under financial obligations to a woman. Not until he reminded himself that her impulse had been dictated by fear for the safety of his father and Tom could he reconcile himself to her aid.

He was nearly at the Flying W boundary before he happened to glance over his shoulder. Then he put spurs to his horse, for he had seen a little group of following horsemen and knew that Sheriff Benson was going to attempt to arrest the wanted Tom.

Hot anger gripped him as he crossed the Woodward range. The cabin had been spared by the raiders and he saw now the reason why. It had already been occupied by Monarch punchers, and Ham Turner quite evidently considered the ranch his.

Benson and his men were still a mile or so behind him when he reached the line cabin in the hills. Hank Gardner and a few others came to meet him and he explained curtly, 'Benson's comin' to arrest Tom.'

'He'll change his mind pronto,' said Gardner. 'The lowdown skunk was helpin' Ham Turner last night instead o' protectin' us. Give 'em hell, boys!'

Rifles blazed as soon as Benson came within range, and he hurriedly swung his party out of reach of the bullets; then, hand upraised in the sign of peace, he came forward at a trot and Hank went out to meet him.

'I'm after Tom Woodward,' Benson announced wrathfully. 'And I'm the law. What in hell do yuh mean by firin' on me?'

'The law! That's a joke, Benson. Yuh're in with Ham Turner to yore neck. Now get outa here and don't come back.'

Benson argued with the irate homesteader and got nowhere, and finally, wild with rage and uttering dire threats, he led his party away.

Kirk entered the cabin. His father and Tom were there under the care of a white-faced Nellie. She exclaimed at sight of him, and he briefly explained that he had been released under bond to appear when the date of his trial was set. Asa Woodward, his shoulder tightly bandaged, was sitting up, but Tom was sleeping. He had been shot through the chest and one of the homesteaders with a crude knowledge of surgery had sterilized the wound and dressed it.

Kirk went outside again and looked about

him. Certainly there was nothing cheering in the aspect. All about the shack crude shelters had been erected with the few tools which had been spared. There were lean-to huts built of boughs, beds of brush with nothing but the limbs of the trees to protect the ones who slept on them, open fires for the cooking. Women and children were sullen and apathetic; the men went about with grim visages. There was not fifty dollars in the bunch and the food they had saved would hardly last two days.

Hank Gardner joined him. 'Yuh won't have to worry about Benson comin' back. He's had his warnin'.' He indicated their surroundings with a glum nod. 'Nice prospect, ain't it?'

'The Flyin' W has cows,' said Kirk. 'We'll sell some at once.'

Hank grunted. 'Where are they? Scattered to hell an' gone. Likely the bunch at Bates' Bottom are busy rustlin' some of 'em right now. And where will yuh drive, and how? Yuh'd be jumped and yore herd stampeded before yuh got off the Flyin' W. No, yore cows won't save us.'

'We own our land. The Federal law won't stand for its bein' taken from us by force. We'll bring in a United States Marshal—'

'Feller, yuh better realize right now what yuh're up against. Ham Turner'll make it his business to see that nobody gits out to bring in a marshal. And even if yuh did manage to slip through it'd be weeks before the thing's straightened out. We'd starve to death before then. No, Kirk, we're licked.'

He walked away, too tired and heartsick to discuss the matter further.

A call from one of the guards drew Kirk to the edge of the trees. A number of horsemen were approaching at a slow trot and leading them was Ham Turner. He waved a white handkerchief and continued to advance slowly until Kirk brusquely halted him.

'I've come to talk with the homesteaders,' he announced.

There was no need to call them; already they were gathering, grim and silent, to hear what he had to say. He spoke at once.

'You men are in a bad way. We have you penned up here and in the end the Monarch can take everything you own. But I want to be reasonable. There are six claims on this side of the creek; I'll pay their owners each a thousand dollars for them. What do you say?'

'I say you have gall even to come here with such a proposition,' Kirk told him. 'I cain't speak for the others, but the Flyin' W isn't for sale under any consideration.'

He looked at Hank Gardner, expecting him to echo his sentiments; but Hank stood frowning and thoughtful and finally spoke. 'Yuh can hold out as long as yuh want to, Kirk, but I ain't. I hate to knuckle to any man, but I'll say right now that if Ham

196

Turner or anybody else hands me a thousand dollars in cash he can have what's left of my place.'

'You're not givin' up without a fight!'

'We've had our fight and we're licked. Look at us! No money, damn little grub, not even a roof over our heads. Our homes are wrecked, our crops trampled, our hay burned. I'm plumb sick of it. I'll take my thousand and pull my stakes.'

'How about the rest of you?'

'I'll sell,' said another settler. 'Kirk, they ain't no use kickin' against the traces.'

The rest of the homesteaders followed the lead of Gardner, and Kirk watched gloomily as the triumphant Ham paid them off in crisp new bills and accepted their quit-claim deeds in return. When he had finished the business and the homesteaders had gone to prepare for their journey, Ham turned to Kirk.

'How about it, Woodward? You can't buck me alone, and I'm prepared to make you an extra inducement. After all, it's the Flying W that I want. You and Tom are both charged with crimes that will result in death for him and imprisonment for you. Sell the Flying W to me and I'll undertake to see to it that both charges are quashed.'

'By confessin' that you had Lane murdered yoreself?' asked Kirk steadily.

Turner flushed. 'Never mind how. I can do it. You'd better take my offer. In your case

197

I'll make it two thousand. I consider it a generous offer, for without you and Tom what's going to become of your father? He'd have to get out and I'd have the place for nothing.'

'You're carryin' a white flag,' Kirk told him heatedly. 'Don't count too much on its protection. Now get out of here.'

'You'll be sorry. When Benson makes his next call you won't have Gardner and his crowd to protect you.'

Kirk made a threatening motion and he hurried back to join his men.

That afternoon the homesteaders set out. They said their good-byes briefly and, on the part of some of them, feelingly. Kirk wished them luck, stonily ignoring their advice to sell out while Turner was in a purchasing mood. Buckboard and spring wagon, loaded with women and children and household goods, jolted out across the Flying W range. When they had disappeared from sight Kirk sighed heavily and went into the shack.

What he was going to do he did not know. Tom was too ill to be moved and his father would be but little help in a fight; nevertheless, he was determined to resist to the bitter end. If it came to the worst he would send Nellie away and the three of them would hold the shack until they were starved or burned out or killed.

He got his rifle and went out to the edge of

the timber where he could see clear across the Flying W range. There he sat as the afternoon waned, waiting for the attack which he was certain would come sooner or later. And then, towards sundown, he straightened and peered towards the creek bed. Two figures were stumbling across the range—an old man and a horse. Tanglefoot Tarberry and Jerry!

Sight of the old man kindled a slow anger within Kirk. Tanglefoot had stolen his last fifty dollars he was sure, for Tarberry was the only one outside of the family who knew where it was hidden. And now the old coot had probably dissipated it as he had the first fifty and was crawling back to bum a meal.

Kirk got to his feet and stood waiting, and presently he saw that the old man was staggering not from drunkenness but because he was very weary. Alkali dust covered man and beast, and once Tanglefoot stumbled to his knees. He sighted Kirk at last and waved a tired arm. The effort seemed to sap the last of his strength; he halted and stood weaving on his feet, his mouth working. Kirk, suddenly alarmed, went quickly to meet him.

'Hy-yuh, Kirk,' wheezed the old man through dry, cracked lips. 'Sorry 'bout that fifty dollars. I jest hadda have it. But I've done returned her with int'rest. That sack—Jerry's back—plumb loaded—virgin gold! Told yuh I'd find her! Rich, boy! Rich—Midas—'

He stumbled forward into Kirk's arms.

CHAPTER FIFTEEN

Kirk's eyes were shining as he carried the old man back to the camp. Placing him on one of the bough beds in the open, he went into the cabin. Nellie was sitting by the bunk holding one of Tom's hands and looking into his wan face as though by the very intensity of her gaze she would draw him out of the shadow. Asa Woodward sat listlessly in his chair, staring into space. Kirk spoke, and such was the ring to his voice that even the semi-conscious Tom opened his eyes.

'News, folks! Grand news—glorious news! Tanglefoot's back and he found that lost claim of his. He brought a sack of ore and half of it's ours. I reckon we can stand up to Ham Turner now!'

Nellie exclaimed delightedly and his father came right out of his chair.

'Yuh mean the old feller told us the *truth?* There really was a claim as rich as he said?'

'Well, old Jerry's carryin' a sack on his back and I don't reckon it's potatoes. I'll be able to tell you more about it in half a minute. Nellie, hand me one of those blankets, will you?'

'Where is Tanglefoot?'

'Outside on one of the beds. He's all in. Nellie, as soon as you can, fix him somethin' light to eat.'

He went outside, covered the old man with the blanket, then hurried to old Jerry. The horse had lain down, and Kirk's first act was to cut loose the heavy canvas sack and roll it to one side. It was too heavy to lift, so he cut the cord which held it shut and some of the ore spilled out on the ground. It was the richest he had ever seen.

He got Jerry to his feet and led him back among the trees. After caring for him he staked him out where the grass was good and dragged the sack of ore into the cabin. With Nellie helping he divided it into two portions, putting his share in gunny sacks.

'What yuh gonna do with it, son?' asked Asa.

'Take it into Mustang right now while it's still light and consign it to the Ocotillo bank.'

'It'll be too bad if yuh run into Turner or Jake Benson.'

'It'll be too bad for them! Don't you worry about me. Nellie, you'll look after old Tanglefoot, won't you?'

He tied the sacks to his saddle and started off, but instead of striking directly across the range he circled through the hills, emerging on the upper road a short distance from Hank Gardner's place. He thought of the homesteaders with regret; they had stood by him loyally only to pull out at the moment when success was nearest. If only they had remained another day!

Glancing towards the pass in the Mustangs through which ran the road to the east he saw two mounted men, and knew they had been posted there by Turner or Benson. They were watching him, but when he turned towards Mustang they made no attempt to follow.

It was dusk when he reached the town, but the evening stage had not arrived and the office was still open. Quickly he consigned the gold to the bank at Ocotillo, which would arrange for the extraction of the precious metal from the ore and credit him with the proceeds. He had kept out enough to cover current expenses. As he left the stage station he met Slim Chance and Tex Evans.

'I'm not forgettin' the way you stood up for me at the JKL,' he told the former. 'In a way I'm sorry you did it, for it cost you yore job.'

'Forget it, Kirk. What I said had to come out and the boys were with me to a man. I tried to talk 'em outa it, but they quit when I did.'

'That's too bad. Barbara needs you. Slim, they're stealin' her blind.'

'Who do yuh mean—they?'

'Rum Blossom Bates—with the help of the M, I reckon. I couldn't tell you before because—well, it was Bates who took Tom in and hid him. But it's got to stop and I aim to

202

tell Bates so. What's Barbara doin' for a crew?'

'Ham Turner brought one in. A hard lookin' outfit, if yuh ask me.'

'Slim, I've had some luck. I grubstaked Tanglefoot Tarberry and today he stumbled into camp with two hundred pounds of raw gold. Likely there's more where it came from, and half of it's mine. My hunch has always been that Ham Turner is behind everything rotten that's happened on this range and I'm out to get him. You fellas want to help?'

Slim's eyes flashed. 'Just tell us how!'

'By signin' on with me as the Flyin' W crew. Now that I have the money I'm goin' to restock and rebuild, and with you boys to help we'll run that rattler to his den and stomp him in the dirt.'

Tex and Slim exchanged glances. 'Sounds good to me,' said Tex.

'We'll talk it over with the other boys and let yuh know,' decided Slim.

Kirk left them and hunted up a man who did local hauling. He gave the teamster an order on a firm in Ocotillo for lumber and hardware and enough supplies to last for some time, mentioning the Ocotillo bank for reference; then he went to the hotel and asked for Vivian.

'How perfectly wonderful!' she exclaimed when he told her the good news. 'Now you can fight Ham Turner with his own

203

weapon—money. Kirk, if you only knew how much I wanted to help you! Financially, I mean. But I knew you wouldn't let me.'

'No, and as soon as my money comes from Ocotillo I aim to get yore check back from Judge Kelly. Vivian, I reckon you're mighty near to bein' an angel.'

Her cheeks colored and the violet eyes were lowered. 'I'm nothing of the sort, Kirk; but I hate and distrust Ham Turner and I blame him for everything evil that has happened.' She went on a bit hesitantly. 'Kirk, I'm staying here at the hotel and it's—lonely. But I want to see this thing through to the end. Could you—would you mind—stopping in occasionally? We could talk and perhaps go for rides, and maybe I'd be able to help Nellie nurse Tom and your father.'

'There's nothin' I'd like better to do,' said Kirk heartily. 'Shore I'll stop in, as often as I can. And you're welcome on the Flyin' W at any and all times.'

He was glowing inwardly when he left her. The world was good. He was no longer a poor nester; he felt more on a footing of equality with this beautiful and cultured girl. A moment later and the world seemed even brighter, for he found the whole JKL crew waiting for him with the word that they were going to work for him.

This time Kirk did not bother to ride a circle; with his men about him he rode

204

directly to the Flying W. The little cabin was lighted, and half a dozen M punchers had made themselves at home in it. Kirk strode in with his newly hired crew behind him and ordered them on their way, and after one surprised look at the capable men who were backing him, they left. Kirk rode on with Slim and Tex to the camp in the hills, and that very night his father and Tom were moved to the more comfortable cabin which had always been their home. Tanglefoot accompanied them, of course. He had recovered sufficiently to ride in the wagon, and as Kirk rode beside him he told of what had happened that night when he had embarked on a brief rustling career.

'I knowed somebody was a-settin' a trap fer yuh, but I don't know who 'twas on account uh because it was too dark to recognize 'em. But I done busted up *that* party by totin' the hide and head to the M, which was where they come from. The fellers, I mean. Now I'm a-goin' after more gold. But fust I aim to do two things: I'm a-goin' to git me a outfit that'll make Ham Turner and Judge Kelly look like a pair o' deuces. I want a swallertail coat and a plug hat and a pupple necktie and yaller shoes. Then I'm gonna rent the hull danged ho-tel and git drunk respectable and stay thataway fer a week.'

He kept his word. He bought his outfit and he rented the hotel and had his breakfast in

205

bed. He treated the whole town to as much as its individual citizens could drink and got gloriously drunk himself. Jerry was stabled at the livery stable and had all the grain and hay he could eat. And on the morning of the eighth day, Tanglefoot, bleary-eyed, uncertain of gait, and once more wearing his desert clothes, got the old horse and started across the desert for his secret mine.

Weeks passed. Tanglefoot returned with another load of gold. Again he donned swallowtail coat and plug hat and went on a spree. Jerry once more waxed fat at the livery barn. And once more Kirk shipped a bag of rich ore to the Ocotillo bank.

Things were happening now. Kirk, working from dawn to dark, set a fast pace for his crew. The cabin was entirely rebuilt and greatly enlarged; new structures and corrals were erected, more blooded stock purchased. As soon as arrangements with the bank had been made, he redeemed Vivian's check and took it to her at the hotel. With him he also took the finest saddle horse he could buy with a rig worthy of the animal.

'He's yores,' he told her. 'A present to the finest little partner I ever had save possibly one, and she's backslid considerable. Climb aboard and let's see what he can do.'

Vivian, the roses in her cheeks, gladly obeyed. If there was anything to cloud the pleasure of the moment it was the knowledge that there had once been a partner he thought a bit finer.

Thereafter they rode together often, and Vivian spent much of her time at the Flying W. Good fortune acted like a tonic on Asa Woodward; he made a quick recovery from his wound, although his shoulder remained stiff. Tom, too, convalesced rapidly under the care of the two girls.

As though determined not to be outdone by the Woodwards, Barbara Lane rushed her own building to completion. In Mustang, the imposing Lane block took shape. The buildings were constructed of brick, freighted in at great expense. The new ranch house was finished, an edifice of Spanish architecture with patio and red tile roof. In it Barbara reigned lonely and alone. Nellie came over occasionally, but her heart was with Tom and she rarely stayed more than a day. Vivian remained away, feeling that Barbara must invite her back if she cared to have her; and Barbara, proud and swayed by a feeling that she herself did not understand, put off the invitation she yearned to send.

Ham Turner was a frequent visitor, of course, and the lonely girl got what pleasure she could from his company. He rode with her, brought her the gossip, and talked for hours on subjects in which she was interested. Always he was courteous and considerate, playing the game skilfully, depending upon time to ripen to the full the friendship between them.

'I suppose the Woodwards are quite prosperous since Tanglefoot found his mine,' she said one day when they were skirting the range on horseback.

Ham had been waiting for her to broach the subject, deliberately refraining from mentioning the Woodwards himself. 'I suppose so, but it'll take more than a gold mine to save Tom from hanging and Kirk from jail.'

'Why hasn't Sheriff Benson arrested Tom? He's living right there on the Flying W.'

'He was badly wounded; I suppose Benson's waiting until he has recovered. No need for the county to bear the expense of caring for him.'

'Could it be possible that he's innocent?'

'I think we've gone over that before. You know the evidence against him; it speaks rather plainly.'

'But Nellie believes in him, and Vivian. Even Slim and the boys.'

'Slim at one time was a good friend of Kirk's, and he was sore when you fired him. As for the others, Nellie's in love with Tom and Vivian with Kirk.'

'Vivian in love with Kirk!'

He flashed her a quick glance. 'Of course. She's always defended him, and even posted bond for him. He made her a present of a handsome horse and saddle and they're together practically all the time. What do you suppose is holding her here in a little place like Mustang when she could be spending the summer at Newport? I think the answer's obvious, don't you?'

Barbara experienced a feeling of emptiness. Something had gone from her. Up to this point, despite her antagonism to Kirk, despite the insults and humilation he had heaped upon her, there was always the knowledge that in some way she held a claim on his affections. They had been boy and girl sweethearts and, as he had reminded her on the night of her party, he had always sworn that she must marry him when they grew up. She had considered the kiss of that night, forcibly administered as it was, a renewal of that pledge; and while she hated him for it there was a pleasurable sensation of satisfaction that she held the power to hurt and still be loved. Now that was gone. Vivian had replaced her in his heart, and as she reviewed what had happened in the few short weeks since her return, she was forced to admit that she had been very blind not to have seen. She had condemned, Vivian had condoned; where she had persecuted, Vivian had praised. Now what she should have foreseen had happened and this strange, new feeling of emptiness had seized her.

During the days which had passed Kirk

had not forgotten his main task: to find the killer of Jonathan Lane and thus free Tom from the charge against him; but there were so many things to be done that he was unable to concentrate at once on the primary problem. One of the first things he did was to have a heart-to-heart talk with Rum Blossom Bates in which he gave that worthy to understand that the rustling of JKL cattle no longer would be tolerated by him. He was pleasant about it, but firm.

'I like to think of you as a friend, Bates. Reckon you proved that when you helped Tom. But it takes a mighty lowdown jasper to steal from two orphaned girls, and I don't figure you want to have a hand in it. There's Ham Turner's stock. If you got to make a livin', steal from him. Steal him deaf, dumb and blind—I don't care; but let the JKL stuff alone.'

He kept an eye open for Sarge Gault and night guards rode the creek in anticipation of the quick attack which Turner might launch at any moment. But a stalemate had developed. Ham evidently was biding his time until he could measure Kirk's strength and find a means of combating it.

One day Slim came to Kirk, his brow puckered in a frown of worriment. 'There ain't been any more rustlin' of JKL beef down the creek, that's certain,' he said. 'But jest the same I'll bet a stack of blues that

Barbara's losin' stock and losin' it fast. I was over on her range today and the place looked plumb deserted. I know there's a lot of square miles for her cows to range over, but I never seen this end of the range so bare.'

'I warned Rum Blossom, and he told me most of his boys had got jobs and had left the Bottom.'

'Know where they went? Over to a feller on the other side of the Mustangs named Cliff Venner. Runs the Box V. And I found out that the new crew Ham hired for Barbara came mostly from that same Box V. Even to a blind man that looks like Ham and this Venner feller are workin' together.'

'You're right, Slim. We'll have to look into that.'

The very next morning they struck out across the JKL, coming to the M wire at the southwest corner of Barbara's range. Letting themselves through the fence, they started a systematic search among the foothills, and finally came to a little park in which were gathered some two hundred JKL steers.

'Jest as I thought,' said Slim tightly. 'All ready to push 'em across as they need 'em. Kirk, I reckon this ties Ham up with the rustlin'.'

'To you and me it does, but there's no proof that he knows about it. His men might be doin' it without his knowledge. We'll leave the critters right here and fetch Jake Benson out tonight. If he's with us when they try to move 'em, he'll have to take some kind of action, Ham Turner or no Ham Turner.'

They rode slowly along the south line of the M, over terrain that was rough and hilly, being careful to keep hidden from any M riders that might be abroad. Close to the southeast corner of the Monarch holdings they topped a hogback, then at Kirk's hasty signal backed their horses away from the crest.

'Couple fellers in that pasture,' he told Slim. 'Couldn't identify them at the distance. Likely a pair of M punchers.'

They dismounted and crept up behind some brush at the top of the ridge, and Kirk examined the men through a pair of glasses. 'It's those two jiggers who're stayin' at Mustang.'

'Yuh mean the rich tenderfoot who says he's lookin' for a ranch and the cowpoke who's supposed to tell him when he's found one? What they interested in the M for? It ain't for sale.'

They remounted and boldly crossed the hogback, but at sight of them the two strangers mounted and rode swiftly away. Cutting the wire, Kirk and Slim let themselves into the pasture, and a short ride brought them close to the cattle. They noticed with some surprise that the animals were wearing the Box V brand.

'Now we *know* Ham and Venner are hooked up!' said Slim.

Kirk shook out his rope and lassoed one of the steers. When he had thrown it, Slim seated himself on the animal's head and they both examined the brand.

'It's a Box V, all right,' said Kirk. 'But just a few days ago it was an M. See those welts where the runnin' iron was used?'

'Well I'll swannee! Kirk, Ham's rustlin' from himself don't make sense. Yuh reckon his crew are changin' brands on him and drivin' M stuff over to Venner?'

Kirk thought for a moment. 'When my father was shot I cornered Ham and he had to explain in a hurry where he was that mornin'. There wasn't any time to think up a lie, and he told me he was on the other side of the east hills lookin' for range. Well, suppose he located over there for himself and is runnin' a spread of his own, usin' a Box V for a brand.'

'Could be. And it ain't very far through that lower pass.'

Kirk got up. 'Turn him loose. We'll have a look at that place of Venner's, but not today. It's too late, and we got business with Jake Benson. Let's ride in right now and corner him.'

This they did, telling Jake not only of the JKL beef penned in the southwest pasture but also of the rebranded stock in the southeast one. Benson scoffed at the suggestion that Turner might be implicated. 'Ham's too big a feller to be mixed in a game like that. If there's any rustlin' or brand-blottin' goin' on, it's the work of his crew.'

'Whoever is doin' it,' said Kirk, 'it's yore sworn duty to find out.'

'I ain't dodgin' the issue none. I'll gather me a posse and come night we'll ride out to the M. I'll stop at the Flyin' W for yuh.'

'We'll meet you at the creek,' amended Kirk, ever mindful of the sheriff's desire to arrest Tom.

When they left the sheriff's office, Kirk spoke shortly. 'I don't trust that jasper farther than I can see him. Suppose you hang around town and keep yore eye on him. Make shore he don't get word to Ham.'

This was done, Slim remaining in town until Benson had gathered his posse; then he rode to the Flying W and reported. 'Not a soul left town but Judge Kelly. He drove out this way in a buckboard. Goin' to the JKL, I reckon. And none of Ham's outfit came in. Benson's on his way now; we'll stick as close to him as a burr to a cow's tail so he won't be able to tip off Ham.'

They joined the sheriff's party and led the way across the JKL to the park where they had found Barbara's cattle. It was moonlight and very still. Quietly they rode into the little pasture, spread out and advanced. Clear

214

across it they rode, their horses at a walk, looking for the mounds that would mean resting cattle. Not one did they find.

'Yuh fellers been havin' a pipe dream, or is this yore idee o' a joke?' asked Benson.

'I don't have to ride around in the dark to make a fool outa you,' answered Kirk shortly. 'Let's take a look at that southeast pasture.'

But even as he said it he knew that they would be just as unsuccessful in that direction as they had been in this. He was right. The southeast pasture, too, was clean, and Benson rode back to Mustang with his posse to all appearances a much disgusted and wrathful sheriff.

Kirk and Slim slowly made their way back to the Flying W.

'It beats me,' said Slim. 'He jest couldn't 'a' got word to Ham.'

'You say nobody left town but Judge Kelly. You shore of that, Slim?'

'Shore as I'm alive!'

'Keno. That's almost as good as findin' the cattle. Kelly is hooked up with the crooked business, too.'

'And him the administrator of Jonathan's estate!' exclaimed Slim. 'The ornery old sidewinder!'

CHAPTER SIXTEEN

The knowledge that Judge Kelly was working hand in glove with Turner gave Kirk additional grounds for apprehension. Just how much power over the JKL estate the judge possessed he did not know, but Kelly had been very closely associated with Lane and undoubtedly held the cattleman's entire confidence. Just how far this confidence extended Kirk discovered the next day. In as casual a manner as he could he brought up the subject with Nellie, learning to his dismay that Jonathan Lane had left no will, but in a letter to Judge Kelly had instructed the jurist to take entire charge of the JKL and to operate the ranch until such time as he thought the girls fit to take over.

This arrangement was almost criminally loose but entirely in keeping with the character of Jonathan Lane. Vigorous and in the prime of life, he had not expected death so soon; upright and honest himself, he was inclined to endow his friends with the same qualities. Under the broad powers conferred by the letter, Kelly could buy and sell, spend or collect, without any accounting to the girls or to the law.

Kirk said nothing of his suspicions to Nellie, but rode at once to the JKL. A

Mexican housekeeper admitted him and went in search of Barbara. Kirk gazed about him critically, amazed and a bit awed at the elaborateness of the furnishings. Here were all the comforts and luxuries of an Eastern mansion. Light footsteps sounded and Barbara entered the doorway. He greeted her gravely.

'Good mornin', Barbara. I've been admirin' yore home. It certainly is handsome.'

'Thank you. I like it.'

'Barbara, I've come over to have a little talk with you. I reckon it'll be easier for both of us if we sit down.'

'Of course.' She motioned to a chair and seated herself. Her manner, if not friendly, at least was not entirely hostile.

'Barbara, we've been at cross-purposes ever since you came home. A lot of it was my fault, I'm freely admittin', and the way things shaped up you had every reason to hate us Woodwards. For a while I let things drift, thinkin' that time would straighten matters out, but now the deal is gettin' so raw that I had to come over and talk about it. Did you know that yore JKL stock is bein' rustled?'

'I know that some rustling had been going on. Now that the homesteaders have gone I'd hoped that it had ceased.'

'Instead it's increased. Outside of an occasional critter for meat, I doubt if the homesteaders ever rustled from the JKL. The

217

crowd in the Bottom were rustlin', I know; but now most of them are gone, too. And still the JKL is bein' stripped.'

He saw the pupils of her eyes dilate. 'Where are they going?'

'Yore old crew is workin' for the Flyin' W, and you know they'd never steal from you. Shab Townsend and Joel Cord and the rest have gone from the Bottom; that leaves the M and yore own crew.'

She stiffened in her chair. 'If you're going to heap more accusations on Mr. Turner, you might as well leave now, Kirk.'

'I'm not accusin' Ham Turner; but he has a hard crew, most of them from the Bottom. Just how much do you know about the men in yore own outfit?'

'Only that they are reliable. Judge Kelly recommended them, and he is administering my father's estate.'

'It's possible for him to be deceived also. Look here, Barbara—Slim Chance worked for yore father for years and he still has a soft place in his heart for the JKL. He made free to ride yore range from one end to the other, and then he came to me and he was worried. Yore spread is bein' stripped of its best cattle. We rode around together, and this is what we found.'

He went on to tell her of the little park at the southwest corner of her range and of the cattle bunched there, and he told her also of

218

their unsuccessful effort to catch the rustlers in the act of running them over the line. Of the pasture on the M he said nothing, for that was not her affair.

'Barbara,' he finished, 'try to forget that we're enemies and take my advice. Order a round-up at once. I know the time for it is a couple months away, but do it anyhow. Take a tally and find out just where you stand.'

She softened perceptibly, knowing in her heart that it was genuine concern for her welfare which prompted the suggestion. 'I'll do it, Kirk. And thank you for bringing it to my notice.' She hesitated for a moment, then went on bravely. 'I've been to blame, too, for some of our differences. I'm beginning to find that the role of—of Eastern society woman doesn't fit me. Oh, Kirk—!' Her lips trembled and her eyes smarted. To cover her agitation she got up and walked to a window. Instantly he was at her side.

'You pore lonely kid, let me help you. I've wanted to all along the line, but things kept comin' up—things which turned you against me. Fire that bunch you got workin' for you and take Slim and the boys back. They all swear by you; they'll get to the bottom of this rustlin' business. Send for Vivian to come back. She wants to but thinks that you feel she double-crossed you. And Barbara, believe me when I say—'

'Am I intruding?'

Kirk stepped back and turned to see Ham Turner standing in the doorway. Barbara hastily dabbed at her eyes with a handkerchief and succeeded in composing herself. She too turned to face Turner.

'Not at all, Hamilton. Kirk came over on business.' She spoke calmly to Woodward. 'Thank you, Kirk, for your advice. And please tell Vivian to ride over and see me sometime. Good-bye.'

When Kirk had gone, Ham turned to her with a frown. 'What sort of advice is he handing out?'

'He suggested that I take a tally of JKL stock.'

'What for?'

'To discover how much of our herd has been rustled. Hamilton, how far can you trust your crew?'

'As far as I'd trust—Say! Has that fellow been suggesting that the M is running off your stuff?'

'He suggested that the crew may be doing it without your knowledge. It's also possible that mine are helping.' She repeated what Kirk had told her about the cattle near the line.

'He's probably rustling them himself!'

She shook her head. 'Slim and the boys would never stand for it.'

His frown deepened. 'I hate to think that my own men would do a thing like that; but if they are, I promise you I'll prosecute them to the full extent of the law.'

'I'm sure you will. In a way I'm to blame. I've been sitting here in luxury instead of attending to the ranch. I'm going to turn over a new leaf, and I'm going to begin by ordering a round-up of JKL stock. And I'll do the tallying myself.'

He shrugged. 'By all means, but I would call it entirely unnecessary. You can't hold your beef herd until shipping time, and that means another round-up later.'

'It means extra work and extra trouble, but I must know where I stand.'

Ham did not remain long, and when he left he rode directly to Mustang and sought Judge Kelly in his home.

'It's time to close out,' he told the judge tersely. 'Barbara's going to take a stock tally. Our turning that gathered stuff back on the range simply postponed the showdown. There are no more homesteaders left to take the blame and Barbara simply won't believe her old crew guilty. Might as well bring the thing to a head right now.'

'In other words, I've reached the—ah— retirement age.'

'Yes, you'd better skip. You've made your plans?'

'Of course. I've mortgaged this place to the hilt and withdrawn all my personal funds from the bank. Together with that little—ah—honorarium you promised, I'll have enough to live on quite comfortably.'

'I'll hand it to you the moment you turn over the JKL. How about your getaway? For your own sake and mine you mustn't be caught.'

The judge smiled complacently. 'You may leave that to me. I've selected a route which is both uncharted and untraveled. I assure you I shall simply drop out of sight. I have the papers ready and my clerk can notarize them without knowing what they contain.'

The deal was consummated in a very short while. A sheaf of papers was exchanged for a sheaf of banknotes. The vultures had stripped their prey!

*   *   *

Back on the Flying W, Kirk sought Slim Chance. 'Get yore rifle,' he told Chance. 'We're goin' to pay a call on Venner of the Box V.'

Skirting the hills, they came to Mustang Pass and entered it. They had not gone very far before they knew that the trail had been used for the movement of cattle from the M to the other side of the range. Shortly after noon they emerged on the far side of the Mustangs to see pastures dotted with cows, corrals, outbuildings and a ranch house of comparatively recent construction. They rode on, arriving in the yard just as the crew came from the mess shack. Among them they reconized Joel Cord, Shab Townsend and several other former residents of the Bottom.

'Reckon you were right when you said they were workin' here,' said Kirk.

As they dismounted before the house, a gangling, horsefaced man came out to meet them. Kirk introduced himself and Slim, explaining that they had come in search of Flying W cattle that might have strayed through the pass.

'Flyin' W? Ain't seen none, but I'll have the boys look out for them. I'm Cliff Venner. Own the Box V. Come and have somethin' to eat.'

They followed him into the house. The table had not been cleared and they saw that two persons had evidently been eating here.

'Foreman has his dinner with me,' explained Venner casually. 'Set down and pitch in.'

They talked quietly while they ate, unconscious of the fact that in the next room, gun in hand, crouched Sarge Gault. The conversation was held to generalities in order that Venner's suspicions might not be aroused. With Venner's renewed promise to keep his eyes open for Flying W stock they left, and Gault joined Venner in the kitchen.

'Strayed stock, my eye,' said Gault shortly. 'They musta noticed that cattle sign in the pass. I got to see Ham right pronto.'

On their way back to the Flying W, Kirk and Slim were exchanging notes.

'That foreman went to work without his hat,' said Slim. 'Unless Venner has two of 'em. Saw one hangin' on the back of a chair.'

'Also the foreman wasn't very hungry; left half his dinner on his plate.'

'Sarge Gault?'

'Maybe. Not the time to find out though. Slim, it all ties up. They're changin' M's to Box V's and runnin' them over here to Venner. Likely Turner owns the spread and uses Venner to cover up. We're gettin' warmer, but it's still a waitin' game.'

'Venner'll report our visit to Ham and he'll have to make some kind of a move.'

'Keno. We'll keep our eyes open. And I reckon it wouldn't be a bad idea to write the Monarch people back East and ask them to send out a man here to check on Ham Turner.'

This he did as soon as he returned to the ranch.

More weeks passed. Cook and bed wagon, remuda and twenty JKL cowboys rode to the extreme northern edge of the range and started their collection of JKL cattle. And with them rode Barbara. She worked with her men, riding from dawn to dusk, sleeping in her sougans in a pup tent, sharing the rough fare. Her white skin blistered and bronzed, the freckles returned, her step become more elastic, her muscles hardened.

As they moved southward the cattle became scarcer and more scrubby. It was increasingly evident that the cream of the JKL beef had been skimmed from the range. Barbara's face grew grimmer, and she no longer laughed. Long before the round-up was completed she knew that her cattle had dwindled to a mere fraction of their former imposing numbers. When the crew finally reached the southern part of the range she left them and strode to the ranch house with the red tile roof and the patio and the rich furnishings that had been brought in at such a stupendous cost. And here Ham Turner found her.

He came into the room with such a worried expression on his face that she knew at once something had gone wrong. He greeted her gravely.

'You're looking wonderfully fit. How does the round-up progress?'

'Almost finished. It's worse than I could have imagined. Hamilton, they've stripped the JKL clean. I've been very, very foolish; I've spent money like water for this white elephant of a house and that row of brick buildings. But from here on there will be a change. I'm going to restock and get back my old crew and be what nature intended me to be—a plain Western girl with a big ranch to

225

boss.'

'Of course,' he said without enthusiasm. 'That is, if—'

'If what?'

He made a resigned gesture. 'I'm afraid—Barbara, I'd rather take a beating than tell you this, but I know your courage and I know you'll not buckle under bad news. You've been on the range for weeks and out of touch with events. I didn't send word to you because I didn't want to slow up the work. Barbara, Judge Kelly's gone.'

'Gone? Gone where?'

'Nobody knows. He disappeared shortly after you started round-up and hasn't been seen or heard from since. I made some inquiries at the Ocotillo Bank. He drew every cent of the JKL and took it with him. Every red cent!'

She staggered as though he had struck her, the blood draining from her face. She put out her hand to catch the back of an overstuffed chair for support. 'No!' she gasped. 'Oh, Hamilton, no!'

He nodded gravely, his eyes glowing with concern and pity.

'It can't be!' she said. 'It just can't be. He was Father's friend; he owed everything to Dad. He wouldn't do a thing like that. I know he wouldn't. He'll come back, I'm sure of it.'

'I'm afraid not. His affairs were in terrible

226

shape. That big house of his was mortgaged to the limit.'

Listlessly she sank into a chair to stare unseeingly through the window. Comprehension came quickly; the cash reserve of the JKL was gone. She had a ranch, some stock, a handsomely furnished and costly ranch house and the property at Mustang.

Ham was still speaking. 'The worst feature of it is that I doubt if you can reach him through the law. That blanket authority your father gave him was so loose that he might as well have handed the outfit right over to him. Of course, he never dreamed that the judge would double-cross him.'

Mention of the law roused her. 'We must see Jake Benson at once. If Judge Kelly has gone with our money he must be brought back and made to return it. I don't care how much authority Dad gave him; it was understood on both sides that he should manage the affairs of the ranch for Nellie and me.'

'I've already seen Benson; saw him shortly after the judge disappeared. He wired all the surrounding counties to be on the lookout for Kelly, but there was absolutely no clue as to where he went. He just dropped out of sight.'

'You think it's—hopeless?'

'I'm afraid I do, dear.'

She got determinedly to her feet. 'There

are the buildings in Mustang; I'll sell them at once.'

'To whom? Besides, they're mortgaged. Oh, I never dreamed that Kelly was the sort of man he is! I thought him honest and upright as a judge should be. When he approached me for the money to build, he explained that he didn't want to touch the cash balance and that beef sales would take care of everything.'

'He got the money from you?'

'Yes. I didn't want you to know. I thought we could handle it between ourselves.'

'Nellie!' she cried suddenly. 'Oh, what have I done? I don't care for myself, but I've lost Nellie's share too!' The light of determination came into her eyes. 'I'll see that she gets everything that's left. Everything! I don't want a penny. I'll sign everything over to her.'

'What is there left?' he asked compassionately. 'If only I could tear up those notes—cancel the mortgage—I'd do it. But I can't. I'm horribly involved. I used Monarch money and I've got to make it good. I've just got to foreclose and get out from under the best I can, and it'll take everything from you—home, buildings, even the cattle that are left.'

It was the final blow. She stared at him for a moment with the despair of utter defeat in her eyes, and if Ham Turner had ever experienced genuine pity, he experienced it now. Then she turned from him and covered her face with her hands. Her shoulders shook.

He stepped forward quickly and put his arms about her. 'Don't Barbara! Don't cry, dear. Let me take care of it for you. Marry me, dear! I'll build a home for you even better than this one in just a little while. I love you, Barbara. You know I do! I want you. Let me protect you and care for you!'

She did not repulse him, but he caught the tiny shake of her head. 'I don't love you. Not—not the way—you'd want me to.'

'Time will take care of that, darling. I'll make you love me. I'll do everything you want me to. I'll see that Nellie gets her share. I'll do that if it takes every cent I can beg, borrow or steal.'

She turned and looked up at him, blinking away her tears. 'You—you'll do that for her—first of all? Hamilton, you promise?'

'I swear I will!'

For the space of ten heartbeats she gazed into his eyes and saw there only honesty and compassion and love. He was a good actor, and this was the finest scene he had ever played. Panic stirred within her, a strong reluctance held her in its grip. She fought both emotions. After all, why not? She owed some sacrifice to her sister whose share of the ranch she had squandered. And Kirk—Kirk was in love with Vivian Stacy.

Slowly she lowered her head, slowly she raised her hands to grip the lapels of his coat. Her answer came almost in a whisper. 'Then—I'll marry you, Hamilton.'

He bent over her swiftly, passionately; but the head remained lowered and he had to be content with kissing her on the soft, shining hair.

CHAPTER SEVENTEEN

Kirk rode in from the range, moody and depressed. Everything was going wrong; Jonathan Lane's murderer was still at large, Judge Kelly had ruined the JKL, Tanglefoot Tarberry had gone into the desert three weeks before and had not returned and, to crown it all, Barbara was going to marry Ham Turner.

Nellie had told him this, together with the story of the mortgages, and Kirk had not yet recovered from the shock. The ruin of the JKL was even more complete than he could have pictured it and Ham's winning of Barbara was a triumph which Kirk had never permitted himself even to contemplate. He had been so sure that she would discover what manner of man Turner was or that he would be able to expose him in time; but she hadn't, and he hadn't, and now he felt numb inside as though something there had died.

He put up his horse and entered the house to find the two strangers he and Slim had seen in the M pasture talking with his father and Tom.

Asa Woodward introduced them. 'Kirk, shake hands with Mr. Sidney Bower. He's lookin' for a ranch. And this is Jim Cole, who's helpin' him.'

'How do you do, sir?' said Bower, and offered a plump hand. 'Just dropped by in the hope that you folks might want to sell the Flying W, but your father tells me there isn't a chance.'

The two were urged to stay to supper, and after the meal remained to have a smoke and a chat; then Bower reminded Cole that they must be leaving. Kirk went outside with them, and when they were out of earshot Bower dropped his mask.

'Woodward, you can forget that stuff about looking for a ranch. I was sent out here by the Monarch Cattle Company, and Cole here is a range detective. The Monarch isn't satisfied with the reports of its manager and I'm here to investigate him. This morning I had a wire instructing me to get in touch with you immediately. What do you know about this fellow Turner?'

Kirk felt his blood leap. 'Gentlemen, I know plenty and suspect a lot more. Come over here by the saddle shed and sit down and

I'll tell you.'

He told them the story of Mustang range since the arrival of Turner. 'The trouble is that I cain't get a single bit of proof that would tie him directly to all the dirty work that's been goin' on. That day I saw you two in the M pasture I had just found a park with a couple hundred JKL steers in it. I got the sheriff and we went back that night, but the critters were gone. Either they'd been run across the line or turned back on JKL range. Somebody tipped the rustlers off, and I know now it was Judge Kelly. He was the only one to leave Mustang between the time I told the sheriff and the time of the raid. I'm positive that Turner was in on that deal, but again I had no proof.'

'Yuh know what was in that pasture of his where you saw us, don't you?' asked Jim Cole.

'Yes. Steers whose brands had been changed from an M to a Box V. We looked that outfit up right away. It's on the other side of these hills and is supposed to be owned by a feller named Cliff Venner; but cattle had been driven through the pass from this range to his, and I'd bet a big stack of blues that the Box V is really owned by Turner.'

'It's a good hunch,' said Bower. 'Turner's undoubtedly building up a big spread at the expense of the Monarch. He's ambitious;

232

already he owns all the land on this side of the creek but yours.'

'He was supposed to have bought it up for the Monarch, but I figured maybe the title was in his name. I intended to look it up some time.'

'He used M money to buy it, but the title is in his name all right.'

'Reckon it's right plain,' said Cole. 'He aimed to run the M plumb into the ground and buy it cheap; then he'd have all of Mustang range but the JKL.'

'He'd have that too,' said Kirk grimly, and told them why.

Bower swore softly. 'He certainly has raised hob with Monarch money. Well, it's time to sit down on him—hard. Tomorrow morning we'll ride over to the Box V. We'll take Sheriff Benson along and throw the fear of God into this Venner fellow. Maybe he'll talk.'

'You'll have to watch Benson—he's in with Turner to his ears.'

'Which is why we'll take him along. Can you come along with us and bring your crew? We'll try to get there just at dinner time, and your boys can keep their eyes on Venner's crew.'

They started out the next morning. Kirk set the pace and they swept into the Box V yard while the crew was at dinner. Slim and his boys rode to the mess shack and surrounded it while Kirk and his three companions went into the house, where they found Venner at the table. He greeted them calmly and asked their business.

'Venner,' said Jim Cole, 'they ain't no use beatin' about the bush. We represent the Monarch Cattle Company. Ever hear of it?'

'Why, shore! Feller named Turner runs a ranch for 'em on the other side of the hills. Don't know him, but I've heard of him.'

'Well, the company's checkin' up a bit, and one of the things we noticed is that a M can be changed right easy into a Box V by simply drawin' two lines with a runnin' iron. Excuse me for gettin' personal, but were any of yore Box V's M's at one time?'

'Why, shore,' admitted Venner readily. 'I bought a few head from Turner—or rather one of my men did. I've never seen the man. And instead of ventin' the old brand and slappin' on the new, we jest drawed the two lines. Easier thataway.'

'You have bills of sale to show for those critters, of course?'

'Shore. In the office. Come in and I'll show 'em to yuh.'

He led the way to another room and produced some papers. Cole examined them briefly. 'They look all right, Venner. I'll keep 'em to check against Turner's records, if yuh don't mind. Mr. Bower will give yuh a receipt for them. Yuh say yuh never met Turner, so I

234

suppose the brands were altered here on yore spread.'

'That's right!'

'Funny, Venner. Bower and I found a pasture over there some weeks ago full of M stuff whose brands had just been changed to Box V's.'

Venner threw out his hands and shrugged. 'I was jest tryin' to protect Turner. Yeah, he changed the brands for us, but what of it? There's my bills of sale; if Turner failed to account for the money I paid him, that's his hard luck.'

While Bower remained with Venner to write out a receipt for the papers, Kirk and Cole went to the kitchen doorway. As before, the table was set for two, but Venner had been alone at his meal when they entered. Once more the 'foreman' had left his dinner unfinished at Kirk's unexpected arrival.

There were three rooms in the cabin, and they had been in two of them. Gault must be hiding in the third. It opened off the kitchen and the door was closed. Kirk motioned to Cole, who followed him to the porch.

'Ham's right-hand man is hidin' in that other room,' whispered Kirk. 'Give me time to circle the house and then tell him to come out. Name's Gault. Watch yourself! He'll shoot at the drop of a hat.'

He ran silently around to the opposite side of the house, crouching so that he could not

235

be seen from the window. Presently he heard Cole's voice, raised for his benefit. 'Come out, Gault, and make it fast!'

A pistol shot answered him and Kirk smashed the window glass with one swipe of his Colt. Then the weapon was thrust through the opening, its muzzle pointed at the back of the man who crouched within the room.

'Hold it, Sarge! Drop the gun and get yore hands in the air!'

He saw Gault tense and half expected him to whirl and shoot it out; but Gault, realizing that if Kirk had meant to kill him he would have done so at once, checked his first involuntary motion and elevated his hands. Cole, at Kirk's hail, opened the door and covered Sarge, and Kirk went around the house and entered. They went into the bedroom where Gault stood.

'Sarge,' said Kirk grimly, 'when I found out it was you who had bushwhacked my father I swore I'd kill you without givin' you any more chance than you gave him, but I've changed my mind. You're goin' to do some talkin' first.'

'Whadda yuh mean—bushwhacked yore father?'

'No go, Sarge. I know what I'm talkin' about this time. I found boot tracks on the bank of the spring overflow. There were two of 'em Sarge, and they were nice and plain. An old stager like you oughta know better

236

than to leave 'em, for I soon found the boots that made them. They were in the M ranch house, Sarge, and Ham Turner said they belonged to you.'

'Why, the lousy double-crosser!' blurted Gault. 'Woodward, I tell yuh I had nothin' to do with it! I come over here the day after the Mustang fire and I ain't been off the place since. Yuh can ask Venner!'

'That's right,' said the horsefaced man from the kitchen.

Kirk shook his head. 'You're not goin' to talk yoreself out of this, Gault. Yuh cain't tell me those boots weren't yores.'

'I'm not tryin' to tell yuh they ain't mine! I'm tryin to tell yuh I never took a shot at yore old man!'

'I reckon somebody got hold of yore boots by mistake!'

'Not by mistake!' Gault's eyes were blazing wrathfully and his face was red. 'Ham Turner wore 'em—damn his lousy soul! He shot yore old man and fixed it so's I'd be blamed.' He swore fiercely. 'It's jest like him; he'd double-cross his own mother if he could get a nickel outa the deal. Kirk Woodward, yuh said I'd never talk myself outa this—well, yuh're gonna be surprised. I *am* gonna talk—and talk plenty!' He stood glaring about him. Bower and Venner and Benson had come into the room. 'It's a long story,' went on Gault. 'Set down on the bed there and

237

listen.'

Then he did a bold thing. Apparently consumed with wrath, he stooped and picked up his gun and rammed it into his holster. The action was so natural that not even Kirk thought anything of it. Bower was already seated in the only chair and Benson and Venner leaned against the wall. Kirk and Jim Cole turned towards the bed.

Gault leaped suddenly into the kitchen and flung the door shut behind him. Running through the outer doorway to the porch, he leaped into the saddle of the nearest horse, snatched up the rein, and spurred for a corner of the cabin. By the time Kirk reached the porch he had vanished.

Slim came from the bunkhouse at a run. 'What's goin on? Who was that jigger on Cole's hoss?'

'Sarge Gault. There he is—headed for the pass! Get the boys, Slim.'

In a matter of seconds the whole outfit was racing for the pass, Cole mounted on a horse requisitioned from Venner. They rode hard but did not overtake Gault, and at the far side of the pass Kirk halted them and gave a few terse instructions.

'Slim, post three of the boys at the pass. If Venner comes through, pick him up. Take the rest of the crew across the JKL to the border. Ride line there to keep Ham from escaping to Mexico. Jim, you and Bower and

Benson come with me. We're goin' to the M.'

They rode as swiftly as their horses could travel, and when they neared the M buildings drew down to a walk, finally leaving their mounts and advancing on foot. As they rounded the M corrals they saw Cole's lathered horse standing outside the ranch house.

'Take off yore spurs,' ordered Kirk. 'If there's anything to hear we want to hear it.'

Silently they crept up to the gallery and mounted it. The door stood open and from within came the sound of voices, one raised in anger, the other placating.

They slipped into the deserted living room, turned towards Ham's office. Its door was closed. They crept close to it, Kirk watching Benson keenly lest the sheriff should make some warning sound. And Benson, knowing he was watched, trod as lightly as any of them.

'For heaven's sake, Sarge, be reasonable,' came Ham's smooth voice. 'I tell you I had to do it, but I never thought of implicating you. I knew anybody could follow *my* tracks; I took your boots thinking there were so many others like them that they couldn't be traced to you.'

'Yeah, yuh did! Why didn't yuh bury them somewhere instead of puttin' them back in my room? I tell yuh, Ham Turner, yuh wanted that shootin' pinned on me so's yuh wouldn't have to split with me! That soft job yuh promised me—where is it? Where's my share of the profit from the JKL steers yuh rustled? And my half of the price of the Box V's that used to be M's?'

'I'll give you everything I promised you, Sarge. Everything.'

'Yuh're right good at promises, ain't yuh? Ham, yuh're a coward and a bungler and I warn yuh they're closin' in on yuh! And now yuh've double-crossed me after I've done yore dirty work for yuh. It was me that rubbed out Lane; me that fired the JKL; it was me that trapped Kirk Woodward in the store and would 'a' got him if he hadn't the luck of the devil hisself! And now yuh double-cross me!'

Kirk gripped Jim Cole's arm with fingers of steel. 'You hear that, Cole? Remember it!'

Gault was still talking. 'I oughta drop yuh in yore tracks, but I'm lettin' yuh go on one condition. Open that safe and dish out every penny that's in it. Do it quick, while I got time to get away, or so help me I'll let yuh have it!'

'Sure, Sarge,' came Turner's agitated voice. 'Sure I'll do it.'

They heard him work with the combination of the safe while Gault continued to berate him bitterly and profanely. Then came Turner's voice again.

'Here's all the money I have, in this box. Take it, Sarge.'

240

Then, suddenly, came a report that shook the room and a harsh cry and Turner's voice raised to a shrill, unnatural pitch. 'And take *that!* Damn you, you asked for it! Didn't know I kept a gun in the safe, did you? Didn't know I could use it? You fool! You triple damned—'

Kirk twisted the doorknob with one hand, drawing with the other. As the door swung back he had a kaleidoscopic view of the scene. Gault was slipping down, chin on chest, arms dangling loosely, knees sagging. Across the desk from him stood Turner, gun still leveled, smoke curling from its muzzle. His face was twisted in a grimace of hatred and his teeth were bared. Just for an instant the pose was held, then he swung his gun towards the door and Kirk ducked.

As he dodged, Benson's gun barrel struck him and he stumbled into the office and fell headlong. He was not knocked unconscious, for his head had been moving before the descending gun, and he twisted as he fell. Benson had wheeled and was barking at Cole and Bower, 'Back! Back, dang yuh! I'm runnin' this show!'

Kirk tried to raise his gun, but his muscles seemed paralyzed. Cole leaped at Benson and the sheriff's gun roared. Kirk saw Cole spin about and drop to the floor; then at long last Kirk found his strength. The Colt in his hand leveled and roared and Benson, too, went

241

down.

While this was happening Kirk was conscious of the crash of wood and glass. He rolled over, got to his knees, leveled his gun over the desk at the spot where Ham had been. He saw only the shattered sash of the window. Then came the staccato pound of hoofs and he knew that Ham had escaped.

CHAPTER EIGHTEEN

Ham Turner rode swiftly, damning the ill luck which had stalked him, damning Sarge Gault who had betrayed him, thrice damning Kirk Woodward who was responsible for the wrecking of his scheme for wealth and power. From the first the fellow had fought him, thwarted him; and now he was done on Mustang Range and must save what he could in the little time left to him.

He was not deceived as to the magnitude of the disaster; Kirk and the men with him must have been listening outside his office door. They had heard Gault's damning admissions and equally damning accusations; they must know beyond all doubt that he had planned Jonathan Lane's death even though Gault had actually fired the shot. Sarge had warned him that they were closing in for the kill; in all probability they knew plenty about his crooked land and cattle deals, and it would require little to connect him with the treacherous Judge Kelly. No, he was done as far as Mustang Range was concerned.

Seething with rage and frustration as he was, his active brain was already busy with a plan of action. The box to which he still clung was filled with banknotes, but there was no time to hide it. He stuffed his pockets with them and tossed the box aside. Money was still king; while he had plenty of it he could buy assistance and, if it came to the worst, freedom. At the Box V were several thousand prime beef cattle; if he could reach Venner's spread, he might be able to bribe the villainous crew to hold Mustang Pass while they were gathered and driven across the line into Mexico. And he would go with them.

He headed straight for the pass, but as his horse leaped from the scrub timber near its entrance he saw that it was blocked to him. He cursed and swung his mount away, while the guards called to him words which he could not distinguish above the pound of hoofs. There was nothing to do now but seek temporary sanctuary at Bates' Bottom. He made for there as fast as his horse could carry him.

Drawing the animal to its haunches before the saloon, he threw himself from the saddle and burst into the room. Rum Blossom, half asleep in a chair tilted against the wall, opened his eyes and stared.

'You've got to hide me and get rid of my horse,' said Ham tensely, and thrust some money into Bates' hand. 'Be quick about it.'

Bates leaped from the chair, thinking swiftly. 'The bar'l won't do. Kirk would be shore to look thar . . . Here! Into Annabelle's bedroom—she don't live here no more.' He opened the trapdoor and Ham lowered himself into the hole. Bates went outside, stripped the horse and sent it lunging down the trail with a smart slap on the rump; then he pushed saddle and bridle beneath the porch and kicked some leaves into the opening.

When Kirk entered the saloon, Bates was once more in his chair. With Woodward were Jim Cole and Bower, the former wearing a blood-soaked bandage. He had leaped at Benson with lowered head, and the bullet from the sheriff's gun had gouged a furrow in his scalp.

'We're lookin' for Ham Turner,' said Kirk. 'You seen him?'

'Heard a hoss pass not more'n five minutes ago. Goin' licketysplit.'

'Hate to question yore word, but—' Kirk drew his gun and yanked open the door to the storeroom. There was nobody hiding there. Next he investigated the barrels at both ends of the bar, but they were empty.

'There's a trapdoor,' said Cole.

244

'He wouldn't be hidin' there. Bates keeps a pet skunk in that hole. We'll search the other buildings.' This they did without finding any sign of the fugitive, and Kirk went outside to examine the ground in front of the saloon. 'A hoss went by here, all right. Ham must have gone to the upper pass or to Mustang.'

They investigated the pass first, for it led to the East and safety, and after satisfying themselves that Turner had not used it, rode on to Mustang. Again they were disappointed; but when the citizens heard the terse and dramatic story there was no lack of volunteers to help run the fugitive down. Bands of men were dispatched to patrol the open range at the northern limits of the JKL, and riflemen were detailed to watch every trail which led from the basin.

Kirk rode with Bower and Cole to the JKL. He would have to tell Barbara, although the thought of tumbling her idol into the dust was distasteful. A month ago he would have welcomed the opportunity; now she was engaged to Turner and, he reasoned, must be in love with the man.

It was dusk when they reached the house, and Barbara had just come in from the range. Leaving Cole and Bower at a discreet distance, he swung from his horse and greeted her gravely, noticing her healthy color, the freckles across the bridge of her nose. He took her by an arm and led her to the gallery, motioning for her to sit down.

'There's something wrong,' she said quietly. 'I know it. You can tell me, Kirk. I guess I'm past hurting.'

He seated himself beside her and rolled a cigarette. 'It's bad news and good, and I'll tell the bad first. Barbara, they've caught up with Ham Turner.' He went on to tell her what had happened, speaking slowly and dispassionately and avoiding looking at her. When the story had been brought to date, he smoked for a while in silence. She spoke at last.

'And the good news—if there can be such a thing.'

'The good news is that likely you'll get back the JKL. Turner evidently planned with Judge Kelly to steal it from you. He'll have to make good.'

'I hope so, Kirk. Not for my sake, but for Nellie's.'

'Nellie is very happy. She and Tom are goin' to be married right away. Gault's confession that he killed yore father frees Tom of the charge and lets me out, too. Now—I'm sorry, Barbara, but we've got to search the JKL. You just rode in and Turner may be hidin' here.' He came to a painful stop, then went on swiftly. 'I hate to do it. For yore sake I'd like to see him get in the clear; but I've got to find him if I can. You understand that, don't you?'

246

'Yes.'

Kirk glanced at her and saw the tears on her lashes. He got up hastily and walked away. If she started crying it would be just too bad; he'd simply have to take her in his arms and spoil everything.

★　　　★　　　★

Rum Blossom Bates raised the trapdoor and spoke to Turner. 'Everything's jake, Ham. They're gone. What's next?'

'Listen, Bates. Go to the Box V and tell Venner to get everything ready to push across the border the minute I get there. I've already planned how to join him.' He lowered his voice and talked rapidly for a few minutes.

'Wall,' said Bates reluctantly, 'it might work. But I'm takin' a helluva chance and it'll cost yuh plenty.'

'You see me through and I'll fix you for life,' promised Ham.

Bates prepared supper for himself and Ham, then started for the pass. It was dusk, and the Flying W cowboys were on guard and had built a fire. They stopped him and inquired where he thought he was going. Bates had an answer ready.

'Got some friends over on the Box V. Now that they've left the Bottom my business is plumb ruint. I'm sellin' out and I thought mebbe they could use a bar'l of whiskey or

247

two. They must be right thirsty by now.'

They permitted him to pass, and he reached Venner's spread by midnight. Ham's orders were transmitted and Bates spent the rest of the night at the ranch. He started for home the next morning and reached the Bottom by noon. Ham Turner was hungry and thirsty and Bates set about to satisfy his wants, then squatted on his heels by the trapdoor and reported the success of his mission while Ham ate.

'Way I figger, we can start in the mornin' and be thar by noon. Venner's gotta have time to gather the stuff. Tomorrer night should see all the critters in Mexico and yuh with 'em.'

Ham spent the rest of the day in his vile prison, for Bates had gone to town to gather news and he dared not leave his hiding place for a minute. At nightfall Rum Blossom returned and reported over the ill-cooked supper.

'It's like I figgered. Kirk Woodward's got the hull basin surrounded and a weasel couldn't squeeze through without help. The hull town's ridin' line, now that they know yuh and Gault's been doin' all the dirty work around yere.'

'Of course they'd blame everything on me!' said Ham bitterly. 'And you, after all the rustling you've done, can walk about a free man!'

'Good thing I can, or yuh'd shore be in a hole deeper'n Annabelle's old bedroom! Me, I ain't smart. I'm just dumb enough to go stumblin' along pickin' up a li'l gravy here and that. Nobody figgers *I* could be gettin' rich with a eddicated crook like yuh around. Now stretch out and git some shut-eye, fer yuh shore are goin' to be right cramped tomorrer.'

The next morning a spring wagon rolled into the mouth of the pass and pulled up at the command of the guards. On the seat of the vehicle sat Rum Blossom Bates and in the bed of the wagon were four barrels.

'What yuh got and where yuh goin'?' demanded a guard, and Bates recognized him as one of the three he had talked with on his first trip.

He grinned disarmingly. 'Got four bar'ls—two full and two empty. I shore had the right hunch the other day. Venner wants a bar'l of whiskey and his boys want one. I'm givin' Venner the empties to use for ketchin' rain.'

The guard had drawn himself over the tail gate and was tilting the barrels in turn. Two were quite evidently empty and the other two were just as evidently full. He dropped to the ground. 'Keno. Get along with yuh.'

The wagon rumbled away, and from one of the full barrels came a thankful sigh. For the first time since the pursuit began Ham felt as though he could relax. When Bates thought it safe, he halted the team long enough to tip over the barrel containing Turner, thus permitting him to stretch. The hours passed and finally Rum Blossom halted again.

'We're gittin' close. Reckon I'd better set that bar'l up.'

They continued the trip, and the accelerated movement told Turner that they were descending the grade towards the Box V. And then from Bates' seat came a smothered exclamation. 'Holy bobcats!'

'What is it?' cried Ham in sudden alarm.

'Shet up!' warned Bates, and the next moment pulled up in the Box V yard. Strange voices came to the man within the barrel.

'What yuh got there, Bates?'

'Bar'ls—full and empty. I'm closin' out and Venner ordered a bar'l of whiskey and so did the crew. The empties are fer rain ketchin'. What's happened to the outfit? Where are the cows and all the boys?'

'Gone. Woodward had a hunch and sent us over this mornin' but we were too late. The outfit's in Mexico by this time.'

'Mexico! What's the big idee? Venner expect me to foller him thar?'

'Wal, he left plumb fast like he expected somebody to foller! Gosh, man, ain't yuh heard? Ham Turner owned the Box V and was stockin' it with M cows. Venner found out that they was checkin' up on Ham and

250

rustled the whole bunch. Good joke on Ham!'

'Yeah? Mebbe he went along with 'em.'

'Reckon not. He'd have a sweet time gettin' over the hills on a hoss and both passes are guarded. No, he's still over on the other side.'

'Wal,' said Bates dejectedly. 'Reckon I had the trip for nothin'.'

He turned the team and started back. Inside the barrel Turner cursed beneath his breath. Venner and his crew had double-crossed him too, and now his position was critical in the extreme.

Just how critical it was he came to realize at the end of the day, when, after much jolting and rocking in the wagon, Bates pulled up at last at his barn. No sooner had the wagon stopped than he heard Bates' indignant voice.

'What're yuh fellers doin' here?'

The muffled reply came to Ham. 'Jest hangin' around in case Ham Turner shows up. What yuh got in them barrels?'

Bates explained. 'Too danged tired to unload 'em tonight. I'll leave 'em here in the wagon.'

Panic gripped Ham. He was in the midst of his hunters, already so cramped of muscle that he was tempted to kick free of the barrel come what may. Every exit from the basin was guarded and he was unable even to reach the sanctuary of the trapdoor hole. No food since morning—no water. Money, yes; his pockets were crammed with it, but you can't

251

eat money, or drink it.

He remained where he was until he was sure it was dark, then leaned backwards and tipped the barrel. The keg tumbled to its side in the wagon and Ham extended his legs, almost shrieking aloud at the agony the movement caused. For many long minutes he lay there, rubbing his legs, flexing his muscles, restoring the sluggish circulation.

It was pitch dark, and as the pain subsided his thoughts turned once more to escape. A desperate plan came to him. Barbara was on the JKL with a crew that he himself had hired. He would throw himself on her mercy. She could drive him to Mustang and beyond the line of guards without arousing suspicion. If she refused—! He sat up in the wagon bed, his lips tightening. If she refused he'd have to use strong-arm methods.

He looked about him, trying to discern objects in the darkness. Soon the moon would rise; he must make his escape now. He got to his feet, an inch at a time; very carefully he put a leg over the side of the wagon and felt for the wheel hub. Cautiously he lowered himself to the ground.

Bates' saloon was ablaze with light, and from within came the sound of raised voices. Ham ducked for the nearest trees, pulled up in their shadow. The door opened and a man came out to stand for a moment watching and listening. He went in again and Ham stole from his shelter. He ducked low and ran across the road, almost holding his breath in the fear of being detected. Into the trees on the far side he plunged, to run like a hunted animal until both lights and sound were left behind. He stopped then, panting with his exertions, and sat down on a fallen tree to recover his breath.

When he had rested he got up and started walking towards the JKL.

CHAPTER NINETEEN

Barbara awoke suddenly. She had slept fitfully, disturbed by vague dreams. Except for her two Mexican house servants she was alone on the ranch, for her crew, fearful of being implicated in the rustling of JKL beef, had deserted to a man. The first light of dawn hung over the range like a gray shroud.

A sound reached her and she sat up in bed, her startled gaze going to the window. On the other side of it she could discern a dim form; fingers were scratching on the pane. She got up, slipped into robe and slippers and crossed to it.

At first she didn't recognize him, for the light was poor and his appearance was not that of the C. Hamilton Turner she had known. She opened the casement a crack and

253

his voice reached her, husky and shaking.

'Let me in, Barbara!' He sagged weakly against the side of the house.

'The patio door—in a minute,' she said, and closed the window.

Dressing hurriedly, she lighted a lamp and carried it into the living room. He was waiting outside the French doors and she admitted him.

'What do you want? Why did you come here?' she asked sharply.

He sank into a chair, disheveled and weary. 'To throw myself upon your mercy—to beg your help. Barbara, you're the only one left who can save me. The passes are guarded, all the trails are watched, armed men are all over the range. This is the only place that is free of them. You can save me. You must!'

She looked at him, shocked by his appearance. The once immaculate attire was soiled by contact with the earth, torn in many places by the chaparral which had snatched at him in his long walk across the range. His black hair hung over his forehead, his face was smudged with dirt and cut by glass from the window through which he had escaped. His eyes held the wild, desperate gleam of a cornered rat.

'You know I can't help you after what you've done. I thought you were injured or I wouldn't have let you in.'

'After what I've done! What have I done?

254

Nothing! Nothing to make a fugitive of me—to bring men swarming after me bent on my death! The law is gone; Benson's dead and I can't appeal to him for protection. Kirk Woodward has set folks against me with a pack of lies, and they'll kill me before I have half a chance to explain!'

'Kirk Woodward was here and told me all about what has happened.'

'He lied, I tell you!' Ham was shaking with passion. 'He heard that the Monarch people are investigating me. That's true! But why are they doing it? Because of you, Barbara! *I stole from them for you!* The money I advanced to Kelly—it was Monarch money. But I intended to replace it—thought the judge was honest! He ran out on me.'

'My father, Hamilton. He was shot—'

'By Sarge Gault! I didn't know it until the other day. I discharged the man right after that Mustang fire. I didn't know what had become of him. He went to a ranch on the far side of the hills owned by a man named Venner. Woodward found him there, but he got away. Came to the M where I was in the house alone and demanded money from me. Told me that he killed Jonathan Lane, but that he'd put the blame on me if I didn't meet his demands. I shot him with a revolver I had in the safe—shot him like a dog! For you again—because he'd killed your father!'

'Then there was Kirk Woodward's father.

Gault said that you shot him from ambush.'

'Of course he did! Of course he said it! I tell you, he was trying to unload everything on me to save his own skin! He knew that Woodward would follow him; I'm positive now that he knew Kirk was listening outside my office door. He was afraid of Kirk and wanted to throw the blame on me! But the evidence against him was too strong; even Kirk will tell you that the tracks he found were Gault's tracks. He knew Kirk was gunning for him and tried to kill Kirk first. He made a mistake and shot the father.'

She stood there regarding him steadily, reading him, analyzing him as a student of anatomy takes apart and analyzes a frog. His voice lost its vehemence; the soft note came back into it; the wild light in his eyes was replaced by that tender, appealing one which he had used to such good effect so many times before.

'Little girl, trust in me, believe me! You've promised to marry me; would I come to you like this if I were everything they have painted me? Would I have the gall to do that?'

But she had finished her analysis, and at last his warped character lay before her in little crooked pieces and she wondered how she could have been so blind.

'I think,' she said deliberately, 'that you would have the gall to do most anything.'

He straightened, his face going tight. The wild gleam came back into his eyes. 'So you don't want to help me, eh? All right—you'll help me whether you want to or not! You're my only remaining hope. Now listen to me. Raise your voice, alarm your servants, and I'll choke the life out of you! I had hoped for at least your pity; evidently you have none. All right, if it takes force to get your help then I'll use force.'

She pointed at the wadded banknotes which showed above the edge of his pockets. 'You have money,' she said scornfully. 'Have you tried buying your safety?'

'Never mind that,' he snapped. 'You're going to hitch up the buckboard and drive me past the guards to Ocotillo.'

'I'm going to do no such thing.'

'Oh, yes, you are! I'm afraid, my dear, that you don't understand yet what kind of man I am. I'm not talking art or books now; I'm talking life and death! You think I'm bluffing. Well, let me tell you this: I was with Sarge Gault when he shot your father. I would have done it myself but that would have given Gault too great a hold on me. I tried to kill Tom Woodward at the same time, but he turned his horse so quickly that I missed. But at close quarters I don't miss. I killed Gault—killed him while he held a gun in his hand. I tell you this just so you won't entertain any illusions about either my will to kill or my ability. Now unless you do exactly as I say, before God *I'll kill you!'*

She shrank back at the expression which came into his face. There was no doubting him; he was that most dangerous of men, a trapped and desperate coward.

'I tell you I can't help you one bit,' she repeated. 'It's simply impossible. The roads are all guarded and I'd not be permitted to pass any more than another person. As a matter of fact, they'd suspect me the more readily because—' she halted momentarily and the painful red stained her cheeks '—because of what people are thinking about us. And you can't hide here at the ranch. Kirk has searched the buildings once, but he's a resourceful young man and he'll search again. Hamilton, why don't you give yourself up and face whatever there is to face like a man?'

He laughed mirthlessly. 'I'm not quite a fool! No, you'll drive me to Ocotillo. You'll tell the guards that you're going there to find out from the bank how you stand. I'll be in the back of the buckboard with a blanket over me, and I'll have a gun within inches of your back. If you tip them off to my presence—give them the simplest of hints—I'll shoot you through the spine and then blow my brains out. Now go to your room and get whatever you need.'

She stared at him for a few seconds, horror

and revulsion in her eyes; but his face lost none of its grim resolve, and finally, with a little gesture of despair, she went to her room. He followed her and waited outside the doorway while she made her preparations.

Together they hooked up the team. The bags she had brought at his command were placed in the bed of the vehicle together with a big lap robe, and he climbed in after them. He had brought her Winchester and a box of shells with him, and these went into the buckboard also.

'Drive at a walk for a mile or so,' he ordered. 'And above all things remember that my gun will never be more than a foot from your back.'

Barbara sat erect and drove, her mind searching for a way whereby she could betray him without bringing about her own destruction. She could think of none. It grew lighter, and presently she put the horses to a trot. Ham knelt just behind the seat, his eyes scanning the trail ahead of them. Mustang came into sight as the sun rose over the eastern hills.

'There are the first of the guards,' he said tightly. 'I'm going to hide under the robe. Remember—one bad break and I shoot!'

He curled up between the bags, draping the robe over him. One of the bills in a pocket worked loose and settled in a fold of the cover, but he did not notice it. His right hand

259

gripped the Colt with which he had shot Sarge Gault, and he raised the robe slightly and thrust its muzzle experimentally against her back.

A greeting was shouted to Barbara, and she replied. He tensed, but they were not stopped. Presently the horses slowed down to a walk and he guessed that they had entered the town. Hoofs and wheels made but little sound in the deep dust; he heard the voices of men, the thud of bootheels on the plank sidewalks, the sound of passing horses. Then the buckboard stopped and the voice of Kirk Woodward came to him.

'Mornin', Barbara. You're up early.'

'I'm driving to the bank at Ocotillo.'

'Vivian's at the hotel. Why don't you ask her to ride along with you?'

'I haven't time to stop, I'm afraid. I—I want to get back tonight.'

Then came another voice. 'What yuh got under the robe, miss?'

'My baggage—saddle—a few odds and ends.'

'Mind if I take a look? This feller, Turner—'

Kirk interrupted. 'Reckon it ain't necessary, Jim. Miss Barbara's word is good. I'll be responsible.'

Turner's fingers gripped the Colt more tightly and his thumb curled about the hammer. First the girl, then Woodward!

'Wel-l-l—All right, miss. Drive on.'

The buckboard lurched into motion and Ham slowly relaxed his grip on the gun. From the back of the vehicle a bit of paper escaped, to flutter in the air for a moment and then settle to the dusty street. Jim Cole saw it, rode forward a few steps, leaned from the saddle—

'Holy cow! A hundred-dollar bill! Now where—? Woodward! It's him! *He's in the buckboard.*' Dust churned as he spurred his horse.

Kirk leaped after him, his face tight. So Barbara was helping the man she loved to escape! How desperate, how foolish, and how blindly loyal!

The buckboard bounced over the uneven road ahead of them, its horses at a full gallop. His own mount thundered a dozen yards behind that of Jim. He shouted at the top of his lungs, 'Don't shoot, Jim! You'll hit her!'

There was a movement in the bed of the buckboard, and they saw the robe flung aside. Ham twisted about and worked the rifle into position; it barked and they heard the scream of lead. Ham rose to his knees, bracing himself against the side of the buckboard. Another spiteful crack and Cole's horse pitched forward, hurling Jim over its head. The man rolled over a couple of times, sat up; then Kirk had passed him.

Barbara looked over her shoulder, a prayer

on her lips. Turner was pumping the Winchester deliberately, swaying with the motion of the vehicle. Kirk was steadily closing, ignoring the lead which scorched the air about him. She saw his hat go flying, the thong which held it severed by one of Turner's bullets. She cried aloud in her anguish; two inches to the left and that slug must have pierced his brain. If only she could do something to help him!

The horses were running free, scared by the shooting behind them. Barbara held the reins loosely, twisted about in her seat so that she could see every movement of pursuer and fugitive. Why didn't Kirk risk a shot! Never mind her—kill that fiend in the wagon!

The buckboard swerved on a bend and she saw Turner grasp quickly at the sideboard to steady himself. And then she had an inspiration! Her lips tightened, her eyes went wider. It would have to be done just right. She turned and took the slack out of the reins. Leaning back, she put her weight on the left line and the team, in obedience, cut sharply to the left side of the road. Instantly she loosened that rein and pulled hard on the right one. The horses swerved to the right.

At the first sudden surge Ham was thrown towards the center of the wagon bed and snatched desperately at the side of the buckboard to save himself; in the next instant he was hurled violently in the opposite direction. He struck the side of the wagon at the height of his thigh and with a strangled cry of dismay was hurled out of the buckboard and through the air.

Barbara heard that despairing cry and looked back. She saw him roll over and over, still clinging to the rifle. She saw Kirk's horse slide to its haunches in an effort to stop, saw him trip and go down heels over head. Kirk kicked free and landed on his feet not more than three yards from where Ham Turner had come to rest. She saw the Winchester come up—saw both rifle and six-gun blaze in the same instant, and with a cry of horror closed her eyes. When she opened them Kirk was standing at the edge of the road the smoking gun in his hand, looking down at the lifeless form of Ham Turner. She fought the team to a halt then leaned her head against the seat rail and sobbed wildly.

Horses came thundering up and pulled to a halt near Kirk. Excited men leaped from their saddles to pound him on the back and voice their approval. Slim Chance gripped his arm hard and said, 'Good work, cowboy! I shore thought yuh were a goner.'

But Kirk scarcely heard them. He was staring up the road towards a buckboard and the huddled figure on its seat. He could almost hear the shuddering sobs. She had loved Ham Turner and he, Kirk Woodward, had killed him.

He spoke in a dead voice. 'Go up there and take care of her, Slim. I just cain't. Reckon I'll have to borrow yore hoss.'

Listlessly he climbed into the saddle and rode back towards Mustang.

CHAPTER TWENTY

He would have continued through the town, but Vivian called to him from the hotel veranda. He reined to the sidewalk, dismounted heavily and followed her into the little parlor. They were alone.

'Tell me what happened,' she said.

He regarded her, utter misery stamped on his face. 'He was hidin' in Barbara's buckboard. A hundred-dollar bill fell out of it and gave him away. He was thrown out and I—shot him.'

Thought of the enormity of the thing overwhelmed him and he sank to a chair and hid his face in his hands. For the first time Vivian saw him give way to despair. 'I shot him,' he repeated brokenly. 'Oh, my God!'

She went over to him, knelt on the floor beside him, put her arms about him. The violet eyes were swimming with sympathy and love.

'Kirk! Kirk, dear, don't! Oh, you can't blame yourself. You simply can't! He deserved it. What you did isn't murder, it's justice. You can't condemn yourself for it.'

He raised his head and she saw in his expression no reaction to her close embrace. He seemed oblivious to the arms clasped about his neck, did not see the devotion that shone in her eyes.

'You don't understand. I'm not thinkin' of myself. I could kill him a dozen times over. It's Barbara I'm thinkin' of.'

'Barbara?'

'Yes. She loved him. No matter what he was, she loved him. She was tryin' to get him away. And I had to be the one to kill him! Vivian, she'll hate me to her dyin' day. I'll never forget her sittin' there, cryin'.'

Slowly she removed her arms and got to her feet. Her face was very white and the light had gone from her eyes. 'I see,' she said quietly. 'You love her, don't you, Kirk?'

'Yes. From the time we were kids on the range together. I told her that some day I was goin' to marry her. And now—' He got up and walked to a window to stand staring out into the street.

Presently she spoke. 'I think that I'll pack up and go back East. I said I wanted to see the thing through to the end, and the end is here.'

He turned then, once more master of his emotion. 'I'll be right sorry to see you go, Vivian. You've shore been a good pal. Yes,

265

we've reached the end—the end of everything. There's just one more thing to do: Bower is comin' into the hotel and I must talk with him.'

Bower entered, saw Kirk in the parlor and obeyed his motion to join him. Vivian left quietly, but she did not go to her room. For the first time in her life she descended to eavesdropping. She stood in the hall close to the doorway.

'Mr. Bower,' she heard Kirk say, 'those mortgages Turner held on the JKL—I want them.'

'Want them? But, my dear man—'

'I tell you I want them. The Monarch has no claim to them; the transaction was a private one between Turner and Kelly. I want them back.'

'But I can't give them to you. Turner robbed the company of many thousands of dollars. His assets have been attached and those mortgages are among them.'

'Are they for sale?'

'Why—yes, of course. Their face value is fifty thousand dollars.'

'It won't do any good to foreclose; the ranch house and Lane Block won't bring half that amount even if you could find a buyer.'

Bower shrugged. 'We'll have the JKL. We can extend the Monarch to include it.'

'It would cost a fortune to stock so much range and the Monarch has been losin' money fast. Bower, I'll buy those mortgages from you. I'll pay you thirty thousand dollars, cash. It's all I have.'

Bower whistled. 'You must want it pretty bad. And if it takes all your money, how will you restock?'

'I intend to give it back to the ones it really belongs to: Barbara and Nellie Lane.'

Bower regarded him steadily for a moment. 'I think I understand. Kirk Woodward, you're a glorious damned fool, but I'd like to shake your hand! I wish I could turn those notes and mortgages over to you gratis, but I'm only the servant of the company. As it is, I'm going to stretch my authority to the limit by letting you have them for thirty thousand dollars. The papers are in the hotel safe and we can close the deal here and now.'

Vivian went swiftly into the lobby and was sitting there when the two men entered. The clerk, having seen all he could see from the veranda, had returned to his post and at Bower's order got the papers from the safe. When the transfer had taken place, Kirk gave his final instructions.

'I want you to hand the canceled notes to Miss Lane, and I want her to think that they were automatically voided by Turner's death. Don't mention me in connection with the deal. You understand?'

'Yes. I can give them to her now. She's just coming in.'

Kirk got up hastily. 'I'll mosey out the back way.' He went to the kitchen and through the rear door. Circling to the front, he was in time to see Barbara enter the hotel with Slim. He mounted Chance's horse and rode toward the place where Turner had been shot. His own horse was loose somewhere around there and he wanted to get the animal back.

He rode slowly, his head bowed. He had made what restitution he could. The check he had given Bower would close his account at the Ocotillo bank, and there was small likelihood that Tanglefoot Tarberry would return with any more gold. The old fellow had been gone for over three weeks and should have been back long ago. The desert had nearly got him once; this time it probably had. And he had put off getting the location of the mine from Tanglefoot, trusting the oldtimer to deal fairly with him.

The Flying W had been greatly improved and its buildings completely restored, but he would have to surrender his ambitious plans to build up and restock. Slim and his boys would have to go, and he and Tom and his father would plod ahead as they had for years, barely making a living. In a way he was glad of this, for the hardships would make his act more surely one of atonement alone.

He rode at a walk along the deserted road. The crowd had returned to town, the body of

268

Ham Turner had been removed. Buried deep in his somber thoughts he had forgotten the horse he had come to search for. The sounds were quite near before he realized that hoofs were pounding the road behind him and that a clear voice he knew and loved was calling his name. His heart stood still. He halted his horse and turned slowly in the saddle. Barbara, cheeks flushed and eyes sparkling, drew rein close beside him.

For a few seconds they looked at each other. So different from what he had expected was her aspect that Kirk was speechless. There was no sign of tears, the corners of her sweet mouth lifted instead of drooped. She leaned from the saddle, raising herself in the stirrups and, throwing her arms about him, kissed him impulsively.

'Kirk, you foolish, foolish, darling! Oh, I love you so much!'

His head swam. It couldn't be true—he was dreaming! Somehow he found her cradled in his arms and knew that he must have lifted her out of her saddle. Her arms were still about his neck and her face rested against his shoulder. The white Stetson had fallen back and hung from its throat latch, and he pressed his face against the fragrant dark hair. If this was a dream he would live it to the last bewildering moment.

'Vivian told me,' she was saying. 'She listened and heard everything. About those notes, I mean. Oh, you wonderful, foolish darling! Eating your heart out because you thought I loved Ham Turner! And I didn't! I didn't! It was you all the time. But I did everything I could to make you hate and despise me, and when at last I realized you were just trying to scorn me into being what God intended me to be I was sure I'd lost you to that glorious Vivian.'

'Vivian?' gasped Kirk.

'I couldn't have blamed you. I'd been so silly! But I've turned a new leaf, really I have; I've been riding and roping and working cows in the hot sun—see the freckles?'

She turned her face up to him and shook the dusky hair out of her eyes, and he looked down at her with all the tenderness and love that had been so long repressed shining in his eyes.

'Precious freckles! They look so good to me that I aim to kiss each and every one a dozen times. And I'm goin' to start right now! Oh, darlin', I never dreamed!'

She laughed softly, tenderly, her fingers straying through the tousled curls. 'Men are so stupid when it comes to reading a woman's heart. Vivian knew. So did Nellie. And when I heard that you took every cent you had in the world—! Dear, you've got to see Mr. Bower and get him to take back those mortgages and give you your thirty thousand dollars.'

'Never in a million years!' he declared. 'We'll throw the Flyin' W and the JKL together. Nellie and Tom are goin' to be married, and we'll be a closed corporation. We'll build up our herd and—' He broke off suddenly, staring over her head. 'Well, jumpin' juniper! Look what's comin'!'

She twisted in his arms and looked. Plodding towards them were two men and a horse. One man was leading the animal, a stout man who panted and staggered with weariness. On the back of the horse was the familiar canvas sack, and walking beside Jerry and urging the stout man to greater efforts was Tanglefoot Tarberry. Barbara and Kirk stared in astonishment until the trio halted before them. The fat man collapsed with a groan and Jerry, with a heavy equine sigh, immediately lay down.

'Hy-yuh, Kirk!' wheezed Tanglefoot. 'Howdy, Miz Barbara! I done fotched yuh somethin'. Recognize it? Ol' Jedge Kelly with the big fat belly! Only it ain't so fat no more; some o' it's done run to lard. Yessir. Come a-staggerin' into my camp one night all tuckered out. Hoss died on him crossin' the desert. Headed for Mexico, he was, and I tumbled to his play right off. And money! The ol' sinner was lousy with it. Most enough to buy our hull claim, I reckon. I done tuk him pris'ner, an labor bein' right scarce, put him to work at the mine. We cleaned up a pile, I'm a-tellin yuh.'

'Tanglefoot, you blessed old coot you!'

Tanglefoot grinned a toothless grin. 'Yuh betcha! Git up, Jedge, and h'ist Jerry to his feet; we still got some travelin' to do. And I'm in a right smart hurry. Soon's I git yuh properly installed in the calaboose, I aim to dress up in my swallertail and plug hat and go on one helluva spree ... Say, Miz, Barbara, how's chances o'borryin' yore hoss—seein' as yuh ain't usin' him?'

Kirk laughed joyously. 'Take him and keep him, oldtimer—saddle and all. Barbara and me are ridin' double from here on and forever more!'

Photoset, printed and bound in Great Britain by
REDWOOD PRESS LIMITED, Melksham, Wiltshire